VANESSA CURTIS

Zelah Green, Queen of Clean

EGMONT

EGMONT

We bring stories to life

Zelah Green: Queen of Clean first published in Great Britain 2009
by Egmont UK Limited
239 Kensington High Street
London W8 6SA

Copyright © Vanessa Curtis 2009

The moral rights of the author have been asserted

ISBN 978 1 4052 4053 6

1 3 5 7 9 10 8 6 4 2

A CIP catalogue record for this title is available from
the British Library

Typeset by Avon DataSet Ltd, Bidford on Avon, Warwickshire
Printed and bound in Great Britain by the CPI Group

All rights reserved. No part of this publication may be reproduced,
stored in a retrieval system, or transmitted, in any form or by any
means, electronic, mechanical, photocopying, recording or otherwise,
without the prior permission of the publisher and copyright owner.

For my husband and my family

Chapter One

My name is Zelah Green and I'm a Cleanaholic.

I spend most of my life on Germ Alert.

Germ Alert is for when people forget to wash their hands and then try to touch me, or when they sneeze on to a tissue and throw it at the bin like they're playing netball and then miss, or, even worse, try to pass it to me. Germ Alert also covers cats, dogs, unflushed toilets, greasy metal poles on tube trains, computer keyboards and mobile phones without covers on, people spitting, kissing or dribbling, coughing or doing anything else with their horrid bodily fluids.

When I'm not on Germ Alert, I'm on Dirt Alert.

Dirt Alert is for when people come into the house from the garden with bare feet and tread bits of worm and grass and earth around the house. Dirt Alert also covers drifting bits of fluff, crumbs, grimy black fingernails, people sweating too much, rancid fat on the cooker, old butter wrappers, smears on plates and windows and layers of dust on windowsills.

Dirt Alert is not as serious as Germ Alert, but it still takes up a lot of my time.

It's a miracle I ever get to school.

The school bus is waiting outside right now, clouds of grey exhaust smoke being coughed into the environment way too close to my sparkling clean windows (I know it's a bit sad, but I had a good go at the diamond lattices this morning).

I'm standing with my stepmother in front of

a mirror with a black frame and gold swirls, like an elaborate Bakewell tart topping. I don't like the mirror, but then again it's my stepmother's taste and I don't much like her either.

There's a big black smear in the middle of the mirror. *Dirt Alert.* My stepmother is watching me watching the smear. She's willing me not to reach out and wipe it away.

My rituals really hack her off, that and the fact that I'm younger and thinner than she is. Mind you, I'm not looking that great today. My face is all red and raw from scrubbing and my black hair is frizzing up and out instead of down.

My stepmother also has black hair, but hers floats in a controlled cloud of black wire around her squirrel-sharp features. She's filled the cracks in her face with some sort of nut-coloured foundation and mismatched it with a red lipstick.

Her hands are hovering just above my

shoulders. I can almost feel the dirt and sweat from her fingertips soaking their way into my pristine clean white shirt.

I've tried for two years to get on with my stepmother and, to be fair, she's tried quite hard to get on with me, but it hasn't worked. We're just too different. She doesn't like my rituals and my stroppy temper. I don't like the disapproval all over her face whenever I talk about Dad or the way she tries to take over where Mum left off.

'Zelah, darling,' she begins. She stops. She's just noticed that I've trimmed all the geraniums in the front garden to exactly the same height.

My stepmother takes a deep breath and grits her teeth.

'I need to talk to you about something,' she says. 'Something important.'

At that moment the school bus honks and emits another explosion of dirty grey smoke.

I can see my best friend Fran leaping up and down as if she's about to burst a blood vessel. *Major Germ Alert.* That would be yet more unnecessary mess to clean up.

I stop my stepmother in her tracks.

'Later,' I say.

I clad my hand in a white tissue as if I'm about to investigate a gory crime scene. Or grime scene, in my case.

Swoosh. The smear's gone from the mirror.

I sling my schoolbag over my shoulder, leave my stepmother doing her daily 'keep young' face exercises in the mirror and run for the bus.

Fran's an awesome best friend. I'm fed up with calling her 'awesome' so today I've got a new word that I found in the dictionary last night.

'Fran, you're such a sophisticate,' I say, trying it out.

A smile creeps over her smooth brown face.

'I'm like *so* knackered,' she says. 'Stayed up half the night teaching my mum how to go online.'

Fran has already placed a sheet of A4 paper on my seat so that my bottom can sit down without fear of dirt. My locker at school is full of pristine sheets of A4 and cellophane packets of tissue. I'm the only kid in the school with an air freshener positioned inside the door.

'I need it back, mind,' she's saying. 'Without an imprint of your arse on it or you're so dead. We're doing sonnets today.'

She's holding out a tube of mints. Brand new and unopened, just the way I like it. I hook my fingernail through a circle of white and drop it on to my tongue without touching the paper.

We suck away in a fug of mint. Fran's cleaned her teeth so that she can breathe in my direction without me fearing contamination. I've scrubbed my own teeth so hard that the bristles on my toothbrush bend back like a demented weeping willow.

Fran's done her usual bus thing of falling asleep within seconds. As the bus takes a tight corner a small hard coconut plops on to my shoulder.

I sigh, remove the head and place a tissue underneath it before replacing it. I take a good sniff of the hair to check that it's clean. It smells of violets, chicken pie and caramel.

I envy Fran lots of things. Like the fact that all the boys in the class go silly and moony over her and she tosses her plaits and doesn't care. She's above all that.

I also envy her being able to switch off wherever she is. I'm condemned to remain an upright rigid ferret amidst a sea of snoring slack-jawed commuters. Sometimes this makes me feel superior.

At other times it's just plain annoying.

Like now. I want to talk to Fran about my stepmother's mysterious words this morning. What is it she's got to tell me later?

A small snuffle comes from the head on my shoulder.

I wish I could rest my sore cheek on my best mate's soft hair, but that's out of the question.

I gaze out instead.

I know there are clothes shops and colourful people and sweet dogs passing by, but I don't see them.

I never see them.

My eyes are fixated by something else.

The smudges on the window of the green school bus.

Chapter Two

You might be wondering why I've got such a weird name.

When I was little and couldn't sleep, Mum used to sit on the edge of my bed and tell me where it came from.

I got my name from the place where my mother lay down in the back of a rust-coloured camper van with my father and conceived me.

When they woke up the next morning, my father tried to cook sausages on a flame about the size of a Bunsen burner and my mother staggered out of the van, shielding her eyes against the sun rising over the fields and went to find out where they were.

'We're in Zelah,' she shouted to my father. He came out of the van, blinking with a sausage speared on the end of a yellow screwdriver.

'What?' he shouted back.

My mother rolled her eyes and gave him her 'affectionate exasperated look'.

'Zelah,' she said again, quieter. 'We're in Zelah. Cornwall.'

She grabbed the burnt sausage and ran away with it over the poppy fields, shrieking like a child. My mother was just eighteen and my father twenty-two. They were running away from their jobs and parents to start a new life together on the Cornish coast. It was the eighties, so my mother was wearing pedal pushers and a white ruffled shirt with big gold hoop earrings and her black hair in a ponytail.

('Yes, really,' she said, looking at my face of disgusted disbelief.)

My father was wearing what he always wore: red checked shirt, jeans and Timberland boots.

By the time my mother turned nineteen, she'd given birth to a black-haired, red-cheeked baby girl. Me.

She looked into my cot at the hospital and remembered that magical night in the leaky camper van on the road towards Penzance.

'Of course,' she murmured, sniffing my sweet, baby-smelling skin. 'Zelah. That's what I'll call you. Zelah.'

And that's how I got my name.

Actually, that's a complete load of crap. But that's the version I believed until I was about twelve and then, after Mum died, Dad came into my bedroom one night and broke down in tears.

'We never stopped arguing even back then,' he said. His fingers were pressed over his face. Hot tears squeezed into the webbed bits between them and ran slowly down his leathery hands.

He smelled of old beer and cigarettes and kept letting out these weird belching noises.

To add to my major stress levels he was eating a bag of bacon-flavoured crisps and every time he opened his mouth I could see loads of soggy potato moving about on his tongue.

Gross.

'Even on the night you were born we argued,' he said.

I frowned. In my mother's version of events, my father was at home smoking fat cigars and ringing friends and relatives with the wondrous news of my birth.

I told him this, trying not to look too closely at Dad chomping on his crisps.

'Your mother always wanted you to think that our marriage was perfect,' said Dad with a big hiccup. 'Actually I was at the hospital all night, arguing.'

With this revelation he shattered another piece of family history to bits of fake plastic in the blink of a hot, wet eye.

I asked him what they were arguing about. Big mistake.

'Your name,' said my father, screwing up the crisp bag and chucking it on the floor.

'I wanted to call you Louise, but your mother said that was wet and boring and she was going to come up with something outlandish and weird, just to spite me.'

'What happened next?' I said. I was keeping one eye on the empty crisp packet on the floor and edging away from my father to avoid being touched by his wet, salty hand. My fear of contamination was new and raw back then. I hadn't yet invented Germ Alert or Dirt Alert.

'She picked up a copy of *Country Hiking*

magazine from the bedside table,' said my father. 'And she flicked through it with her eyes shut and then she stabbed her finger down on to the page.'

He hiccupped again and stabbed his own finger hard on to my leg at that point. I winced but said nothing.

'She opened her eyes and her finger was on the word "Zelah"' said my father. 'And that was it. That's what she called you.'

'Oh,' I said. I felt flat and cross and very much in the present day. 'So you didn't come up with the idea in Cornwall on a romantic camping holiday, then?'

'Nope, sorry,' said my father. 'We never camped. And whilst I'm ruining all your childish illusions I might as well tell you that you were conceived in a damp council flat in Deptford. We had cockroaches.'

Then he blew his nose (I ducked under the

sheet to avoid droplets) and left me sitting up in bed with my sense of identity lying in pieces around me.

There was nothing safe or solid any more. My past was a fraud, my name was rubbish, my mother was dead and my father was drinking too much beer, eaten up with regret and guilt.

That's when the rituals began to take over my life.

I suppose I ought to explain exactly what they are.

Chapter Three

My rituals are all part of Germ Alert and Dirt Alert.

These are some of my rituals.

You might think they sound a bit crazy, but to me they're normal, just something I have to do before I can leave the house. It's a pain if I'm running late for school, but I have to do them or else the whole day goes wrong and I get hot and anxious and can't concentrate on anything.

My rituals change a bit depending on what music I'm listening to. At the moment I'm listening to Green Day. Just as the first track finishes I step into the bathroom. Then I've got four tracks to get my hands done. To get them properly clean I have to wash them thirty-one times each, right hand then left. On a good day I finish this just as the fifth track comes to an end. On a bad day I forget and touch the toilet by mistake as I'm reaching for the towel. That means I have to wash them another thirty-one times, which takes me to the end of track eight. After my hands I load up a nailbrush with clean white soap and scrub my face until it's raw. Then I have the tenth track to put my clothes on and get my hair brushed. I brush it thirty-one times using downwards strokes. At the end of all this it still looks like a mad black bush but that's not really the point. I try to tie in the last brush stroke with the last note of track eleven. I never get to track twelve. If I do, it's bad luck for the entire day and people I love might get run over or fall off a cliff, so I make sure this doesn't happen. I once got to track twelve when

I was listening to the Kaiser Chiefs, but their songs are shorter so I told myself that that was OK.

I do one hundred and twenty-eight jumps on the top step and then I go downstairs, changing my shoes on the bottom one.

Once I've gone down for breakfast I can't go upstairs or I'll have to start the whole washing thing over again.

This is really annoying when I leave my school bag upstairs. If my stepmother has already gone to work, then I'm stuffed.

Teachers don't like 'Sorry, Miss, I couldn't go upstairs to get my homework or else I'd have had to wash my hands thirty-one times' as an excuse.

This is another one of my rituals:

Wardrobe spacing.

I go mental if anything is touching the item hanging next to it. There has to be a gap of at least four centimetres between each piece of clothing, and I keep a ruler in the cupboard just in case so I can measure the gaps and woe betide if anyone gives me a piece of new clothing because that screws up all the measurements and I usually end up having to give it back to them, which is rude, or else I wrap it in tissue paper and put it on a shelf in the top.

The last thing I have to do before I go to school is this:

Checking. This is my checklist for checking:

Check kettle switched off. (Up to ten times.)

Check back door locked. (Up to ten times.)

Check no crumbs on kitchen worktop. If there are, put on plastic gloves and wipe them away with a clean tissue. Throw away tissue without touching bin. If touch bin, wash hands thirty-one times, left then right.

Check that labels on jars, bottles and tins are all lined up in the cupboard and facing the front.

Check television switched off at mains.

Check all lamps switched off.

Make sure curtains pulled open and exactly same distance apart.

Check all windows are locked.

That's my morning rituals and my checks. My evening rituals take place when I get home from school. This is what I have to do:

Change from school shoes into flip-flops on bottom stair.

Go upstairs not touching banister.

Jump one hundred and twenty-eight times on top step.

Have shower.

Change out of school uniform.

Wash hands another thirty-one times, first left, then right.

If I go to the toilet after that the whole hand-washing thing has to be done again.

Do homework in bedroom.

Jump one hundred and twenty-eight times on top step.

Go downstairs not touching banisters and change shoes on bottom step.

That's all of my rituals.

After I've done all my rituals I usually manage to have a pretty normal evening until I have to go to bed at ten, when the whole washing thing starts up again. Most of the time I cope OK with my 'little problem'. There aren't many people around to be annoyed by it. Mum's dead and my stepmother's out as much as possible.

Oh yes. And just over four weeks ago my dad vanished off the face of the planet. Picked up his briefcase one day and air-kissed me goodbye to avoid major Germ Alert. He smelled of leather and aftershave and wood chippings and that weird dried shampoo stuff, just like normal.

YA/2166192

Dad got into his car and drove off to his teaching job at school. And he never came back.

Which is why I've been stuck in this house with my vile stepmother for the last month.

So, Fran's the only one who sees me close up on a daily basis and she's brilliant. Fran's mum is cool about it too. When they invite me for tea, they let me take my own knife and fork to avoid washing problems.

'There's nothing wrong with wanting to be clean and tidy,' says Fran's mum.

I've noticed something about Fran's mum when she says this.

She never looks me straight in the eye.

School's out and I'm home again.

I change out of plimsolls, do jumps and get into the shower to scrub off the smells of chalk, sweat and rubber gym shoes. My stepmother is downstairs, murmuring on the phone.

She knows that this means I'll have to disinfect the mouthpiece again, but she doesn't care.

I pad into my room wrapped in a soft, white towel and open the wardrobe to find a clean T-shirt.

I freeze.

My wardrobe is almost empty. There are only two items left hanging in front of me – a long, red gypsy skirt with flippy chiffon layers and a rose-coloured sleeveless summer dress with tiny embroidered red flowers round the waist.

Both these things are for wearing on special occasions. Dad bought them for me. He was pretty bad at buying clothes for girls, but he consulted our next-door neighbour Heather on this occasion and she knows what I like.

All my ordinary clothes have vanished, save for a T-shirt and jeans laid out across my bed in the shape of a long, thin, flat person.

I go to the top of the stairs.

'Chan-tal!' I shout down. My stepmother is half French, although you'd never know it from her squeaky voice and shocking taste in clothes.

'Got to go – she's noticed,' she murmurs, replacing the handset.

'Yes,' I say. 'I have noticed. Where are all my clothes?'

Chantal pauses at the foot of the stairs with her hand on the banister. She doesn't speak.

She doesn't need to. Behind her, plonked on the red-and-white tiled floor, is a suitcase.

My suitcase.

Outside I can hear the sound of an engine running.

I hold on to the wall with my tissue, giddy. I am still wearing the bath towel with another wrapped around my wet hair.

'Zelah, get dressed at once,' says my step-mother. 'I was meaning to tell you earlier but you rushed off to school.'

24

'Tell me what?' I say. I am trying to decipher the expression on her face as it stares up at me. Guilt? Worry? Excitement?

No. Relief. That's it. My stepmother looks relieved. As if she has been relieved of a huge burden.

The burden appears to be me.

I get dressed in a daze. I don't bother to blow-dry my hair or put on any make-up. All the time my stepmother hovers around my bedroom, glancing at her watch and out of the window to where an engine can still be heard running.

My mind works overtime as I pull on my jeans. What if I tie myself to the bed and refuse to move? Or push her out and lock the door? Who's waiting in the car outside?

I zip up my flies and turn to face her.

'Well, come on,' I say. 'Don't I deserve to know what's happening?'

My stepmother takes a step towards me. Her eyes are large and imploring and to my amazement, filled with tears. I have never seen her cry, not even on the night when Dad left us.

'I've arranged for you to go away for a while,' she says. 'I can't cope with your little problem any more.'

Of course. Her tears are not for me, they're for her.

'And also,' she says. 'I'm getting quite stressed out by trying to cope with you. All my confidence is going. I'm ageing too fast, you know.'

I sink down on the edge of the bed and stare at her.

'You're joking, right?'

It's obvious that she's deadly serious.

'I've asked Heather to take you away,' she says. 'You'll be gone for about a month. After that you might be able to come home again.'

'You're booting me out?' I say. 'You're booting me out and you haven't even got the guts to drive me there yourself?'

I pull back the net curtains. Heather Huntsman is waiting in her red car outside, tapping her fingers on the steering wheel. Heather's lovely – much lovelier than my stepmother, in fact – but that's not the point.

'Zelah, this is upsetting for me too,' says Chantal. She ignores my loud snort of anger. 'But we need to get you treated. Come on.'

She gestures me off the bed and shoos me towards the door. I can't help noticing that she's leaving a small trail of mud on the white carpet – she forgot to change into her indoor shoes – but Dirt Alert is starting to fade next to the great big whopping new problem now facing me.

'I'm fourteen,' I say as she hustles me downstairs and grabs the suitcase. 'Fourteen.

I'm too young to leave home! Where are you sending me? What would Dad say if he knew what you were doing? How will he know where to find me?'

She ignores me and hurries me towards where Heather is waiting, throws my bag into the boot and pushes me into the back seat.

The engine starts and we leave her there, a tall awkward figure, standing in silence and hugging her own elbows.

She doesn't wave goodbye.

Chapter Four

Heather gives me a quick appraising glance. 'Seatbelt,' she says as we roar off in a cloud of Porsche-induced fug.

'Can't,' I say.

I don't trust belts in Other People's Cars. They've been on Other People's Bodies, absorbing bits of dead skin and old sweat. A bit of the belt might touch the exposed area of my chest and neck and then I'll have to scrub myself raw.

'God Almighty,' says Heather. 'As if this isn't stressful enough already.'

She screeches to a halt at the foot of our road.

The cigarette lighter pops out with a loud click. Heather sucks in her cheeks while the lighter glows red. She puffs on the fag as if the next forty years of her life depend upon it, although at this rate she probably won't live to see many of them.

Bits of dirty ash flutter and splutter towards the passenger seat.

Dirt Alert.

She sees my face of angst and smokes out of the window instead.

I flush with shame. Heather's been our neighbour for ages and I like her a lot. Mum liked her too. When Mum started to get sick, Heather was brilliant. She went shopping for Mum and bought clothes for her. She treated Mum to little bits of colourful jewellery to cheer her up and bought special organic foods to tempt her into eating more.

Even my stepmother must like Heather, or

why else would she rope her into taking me away?

I'm never sure whether Heather likes my stepmother, though. She's polite and smiley in our house, but I sense something tight shifting and wriggling underneath.

'OK, kiddo,' Heather's saying. 'Here's the deal. Your stepmother wants me to drive you to the local hospital for treatment, but we can't go anywhere until you put your seatbelt on.'

I gulp at the word 'hospital', but look around the car. There's a box of Kleenex on the back seat.

'Sorted,' I say.

I wrap wads of tissue round the seatbelt, enough to ensure there's no area of pale chest skin left uncovered.

'Good girl,' Heather says. She starts the engine, tosses her fag butt out of the window and lowers her dark designer sunglasses from where they've been perching on her head.

Heather's gorgeous. She's only five years younger than my stepmother, but she looks about twenty years younger. She's got this long, red hair with honey-coloured highlights woven through it and it kind of flips forward over her eyes until she pins it into place with the sunglasses. She's tanned, tall and skinny and works as a fashion journalist in London.

Mum and Heather used to go shopping for hours. They called themselves 'ladies who lunch' and they'd come home tipsy with armfuls of boxes and bags and pour white wine into long-stemmed glasses. Then they'd sit in the garden smothered in sizzling coconut gunk and hoot with laughter, teasing Dad and me.

Dad used to give Heather admiring looks when he thought that Mum and me weren't looking. Mum used to tease him about it and say, 'Typical man!'

Besides, Mum was just as pretty as Heather in a different sort of way. Dark curls instead of long red-blonde hair. Red cheeks instead of tanned ones. Mum was all curvy and feminine, but Heather was as thin as a stick insect's inside leg. Mum wore combats and little vest tops. She had an outdoorsy daytime sort of look. Heather wore micro mini-skirts and tight jeans. She looked as if she only came alive at night inside a trendy wine bar perched on a high barstool with lots of men ogling her.

'Why aren't you married?' I ask Heather. I'm trying not to think about the hospital.

She's driving with assurance, her long brown arms tipping the steering wheel this way and that, leaning her head back against the headrest, tapping one foot to the radio.

'It's not the most important thing in life,' she says. That's a typical Heather answer. It leaves other questions begging to be asked.

I think about asking Heather if I can live with her instead of going to the hospital, but I already know what the answer will be.

'I'm a career woman,' she'll say. 'I mean – love you, and all that, but I'm just not cut out for looking after kids. What would happen to my gorgeous nails? Do I look like your typical mother?'

Heather's squeezed into a red sleeveless top today and black skinny jeans. She looks like a teenager.

Her nails end in perfect scarlet tips with not a chip in sight.

I stick a tissue behind my head so that I can lean it back without fear of getting my hair dirty, and watch the brown concrete walls of our local hospital loom into view. It's a converted Victorian lunatic asylum. Appropriate. My stepmother's always telling me I'm crazy.

'They won't chain my head and legs to the

wall or anything, will they?' I say. My heart is starting to pound beneath the wads of tissue. I miss Dad so much that there's a great panging ache washing up my legs towards my head.

'Nope,' says Heather. 'That I can guarantee you.'

We've got caught in a traffic jam just outside the hospital gates.

'You're in the wrong lane,' I point out. 'You need to turn left in a minute.'

Heather has developed selective deafness. She turns up the volume on the radio and a jangly blast of Madonna blares out, all booming bass. The car windows vibrate and a man in the car next to us smirks at Heather and does a horrid wink.

Heather taps her nails on the outside of the car door. She's bawling at the top of her voice to the Madonna song.

She ignores the man.

The lights change. Heather puts her foot on the accelerator and screeches away, staring straight ahead and singing like a maniac.

The hospital becomes a small brown dot in my wing mirror.

'Erm,' I say. A small knot of fear is growing in my stomach. Has she gone mad? Is she kidnapping me? Where are we going? At least the hospital would have been nice and clean with lots of good disinfectant and bleach.

'I love that song,' says Heather as Madonna reaches her climax and is cut off by the prattling drone of a DJ. 'Fifty and she's still got the body of a sex goddess, the cow.'

Heather's hair whips around her face like red spaghetti as we join a busy road. Every now and then she pushes it back behind her ears and then a few strands break free again, starting a mutiny until the whole lot flips out and whams her in the face.

'Note to self, bring hair clip next time,' she laughs. The frowning snappiness has vanished, to be replaced by a vibrant pair of grinning red lips. I feel a bit plain sitting next to Heather, even though I quite like my own mop of hair and I've got very long legs. But Heather looks like a film star.

We're driving down a dual carriageway at breakneck speed and the tissues are flying off my chest in the breeze and Heather is still not telling me where we're going.

'The hospital's back the other way,' I say, just in case she's truly flipped and failed to see the enormous building.

'I know, I know, it's off down the road we go,' sings Heather. She ferrets about in the glove compartment without taking her eyes off the road and chucks a sandwich at me. It's my favourite sort, one of those ones in a lovely clean, sealed, plastic triangle.

I sigh and shake my head. She really has lost it, I reckon.

I peel off a cellophane corner and sink my teeth into soft tuna and cucumber mayo.

There doesn't seem to be anything else I can do.

Three hours later Heather swings off the A30, navigates a couple of roundabouts and turns into a long street studded with tall white Victorian houses. Daylight is fading to a birdsong-soaked twilight.

'What is this?' I say. 'Why are we here?'

Heather is brushing her hair back into a sleek wave of red and gold.

She pushes her glasses back on to her head and turns to face me.

'I couldn't take you to that hospital,' she says. 'I don't think it was the right place for you.'

'But my stepmother told you to take me

there,' I say. 'She'll go mad when she finds out.'

Heather juts out her chin and gives me her stubborn look.

'I'll keep her off the track for a while,' she says. 'Your father wouldn't want you to go to that hospital.'

'How do you know?' I say.

We fall silent for a moment. It's been over a month since I last heard from Dad. Nobody seems to know where he's gone. The head-mistress of the school where Dad taught has rung home about a million times complaining about having to get in emergency supply teachers at short notice.

Heather is waving at somebody. A tall figure in a white apron has appeared at the top of a flight of stairs and is waving back.

'Who's that?' I say. This is all becoming a bit much. It's been hours since I've washed and I feel grimy and hot and numb from the car seat.

'That,' says Heather, grinning, 'is Erin. She's like a big sister to me. Come on.'

She leaps out of the car and pulls my suitcase from the tiny boot of her car.

I straggle behind, removing bits of tissue from my front. I kick shut the car door to avoid touching it with my hands.

Heather is embracing the woman at the top of the steps. As they hug they bounce up and down like excited kids. Heather slips the woman some sort of folder. I can't see what's in it, but I catch a glimpse of my name written in black marker pen across the front.

I wait for them to finish, shifting from my right leg to my left. The cracked black and white diamond tiles I'm standing on look just right for jumping on. I could do with a good jump, but I'm not giving in to my 'little problem' in front of a complete stranger.

The woman steps forward. She's wearing a

shapeless white linen shirt over a long grey cotton skirt. Her apron has a bold picture of a red chilli pepper on it and says 'Hot Stuff!'. She has dishevelled dark-brown curly hair, shot through with grey, and a face not smooth like Heather's, but lined and brown. She must be at least ten years older than Heather, but when she smiles at me, her eyes crinkle up at the corners.

'I'm Erin,' she says. 'I won't shake your hand, Zelah. I don't want to stress you out straight away.'

I have no idea what to say to this as I'm already pretty stressed out by the weirdness of everything, but the woman looks OK. Heather is gesturing for me to step inside, so I walk in behind her.

There's a gold plate by the front door. It says 'Forest Hill House'.

Just as the door shuts behind us, the most unbelievable thing happens.

There is a scream from somewhere upstairs. The loudest scream I've ever heard. The sort of scream I would make if I were being throttled by a pair of naked hands, or if I'd just found Fran with her neck slit open by a dirty knife, or somebody was sticking burning hot pins into my eyeballs without sterilising them first.

The scream is followed by the sounds of footsteps running, doors opening and shutting and a low adult voice trying to calm the screamer down.

Even Heather loses her confident grin for a moment. She freezes. She stares at me, wide-eyed. We both goggle like scared rabbits in the direction of the scream.

The woman with the curly hair never stops smiling for a second. She looks as if she's caught the faint tinkle of heavenly bells rather than the heart-stopping screech that we've just heard.

'Don't worry, it's Caro having one of her

expressive moments,' she says. 'Sounds far worse than it is.'

I want to reach for Heather's hand but I can't. I've got no gloves and I've run out of tissues.

Heather's glancing at her watch and biting her lip.

'You're not going, are you?' I say. 'Can't you just stay for a bit longer?'

'Sorry, kiddo,' she says. 'I've got a date tomorrow morning with a rack of black gothic puffball skirts.'

She makes as if to grab my shoulders, remembers just in time, blows me a gentle air-kiss involving as little breath as possible, hugs the tall woman again and bounds down the steps towards her Porsche.

'You'll be fine here,' she calls over her shoulder, throwing her Gucci bag into the back of the car and easing her slim frame into the driving seat.

She revs up the engine and roars back off to her other life, leaving a cloud of thick grey smoke hovering in the street.

It's like my last link with Mum and Dad has just vanished.

The woman clicks the heavy front door shut behind me and locks it. The sound echoes in the tiled hall.

'I expect you'd like to see your room,' she says.

It isn't a question and, in any case, I wouldn't know how to answer it.

The banisters are brown and smooth and made of polished oak.

I can detect the smear of recent fingerprints. *Dirt Alert.*

I tuck my elbows into my sides and shove my hands into my pockets.

It's too late for escape now.

I follow the woman upstairs.

Chapter Five

Erin leads me up two flights of stairs, past lots of doorways.

Some of the doors are closed. Others give a flash glimpse of unmade beds, posters, the flicker of television screens, desks and heaps of washing. The whiff of perfume, sweat, bubble bath and stale burgers hangs around the hall.

'Wednesday night we have takeaway,' says Erin, reading my mind. 'It's our way of telling them they're doing well.'

Well at what?

I can tell from the rooms I've passed that this isn't a hospital. There's too much mess.

Hospitals smell of disinfectant and bleach. This house smells of teenage life.

We've reached a smaller flight of stairs at the very top of the house. Erin bustles up them, jangling a bunch of keys in her hand. Her bulk fills the narrowing stairwell. Childbearing hips, as Heather would say.

She leads me into a room bursting with light. The floorboards have been painted white and the chest of drawers by the bed is a pale yellow. White curtains flap in the breeze, like a room overlooking a big blue sea somewhere. Except that this room overlooks the untidy front garden of the house opposite. Unlike the rooms I just saw downstairs, this one is clean. Tidy.

My eye buzzes around the furniture and alights upon a tiny sink in the corner of the room and a rack of clean white towels.

I glance at my watch. Nine thirty-five. I'm already running late for my bedtime rituals. Erin shows no signs of leaving. She's sitting on the edge of a small neat white bed and patting for me to come and sit next to her.

A slight sweat breaks out on my face. *Dirt Alert.*

Everything is out of sync. For all I know, one of the taps won't work. That will screw up the whole washing thing. If I can't wash on time, I can't get to bed and go to sleep.

'Don't worry, I'll leave you to settle in soon,' says Erin. Her habit of reading my mind is starting to unnerve me.

'It's OK, I didn't mean . . .' I mumble, flushing.

Erin is beaming at me from behind her small round glasses.

'You must be wondering what this is all about,' she says. 'Did Heather tell you anything?'

My mind flashes back to the car journey and Heather's hair whipping around. Her long tanned fingers on the wheel and her loud, out-of-tune singing.

It seems a lifetime ago.

I'm itching for Erin to go. There's a piece of grey fluff drifting over the white floorboards. Uh-oh, *Dirt Alert* again. If I don't pick it up before it gets to my feet, I'm going to have a major panic attack.

Erin follows my eyes. She gets up and squashes the piece of fluff between finger and thumb before shoving it in her apron pocket.

My stepmother wouldn't even have noticed.

'Thanks,' I say. I fiddle with my fingernails, ease out a piece of dirt from underneath one of them.

Erin laughs.

'No need to thank me,' she says. 'It's my job.'

I must have looked blank at this.

'I'm a doctor specialising in the treatment of teenage disorders,' she says. 'In fact, the others call me "the Doc" around here. You've been sent here because of your Obsessive Compulsive Disorder.'

I give a little jump and have to refrain from looking around to see if she is speaking to someone else. I know that my rituals have a medical name, but I prefer not to use it.

This is one of my beliefs:

Giving something a name makes it more real.

When Mum got cancer we never called it 'cancer' at home. We called it 'this dratted thing', or 'the situation'. It was only when she was admitted to hospital that the word leapt up and smacked us in the face. A 'cancer care nurse' made Mum more comfortable. A doctor said that the 'cancer had progressed two stages'. A healer visited Mum and told her to 'visualise her cancer cells being beaten into submission.' Once the word got out, it followed us home and got into our nightmares and Mum's bloodstream.

Then it killed her.

That's why I don't like giving things a name.

The Doc gets up, pressing her hands into the small of her back like pregnant people do, stretching with a grimace.

'Long day,' she says. 'I'll let you get a good night's sleep and in the morning I'll introduce you to the others.'

Although I saw those bedrooms downstairs, a small thrill of fear grips my stomach.

'Don't worry about them,' says the Doc. She's starting to seriously freak me out now. I wonder if I'm speaking my thoughts out loud without realising it.

'It's a quiet month,' she says. 'We've only got four kids in at the moment, plus Josh and me make six. Seven, if you include Sneezer. He's the cat.'

I'm too tired and wired to ask who Josh is.

And I hate cats. They carry a lot of germs.

As soon as her tall figure passes through the doorway I rush to the sink.

I wrap a tissue round the left-hand tap and twist. With a small squeak it jets out a stream of warm water. I wash my right hand thirty-one times. I grab the sliver of cream-coloured soap and scrub my face with my right hand until it is red and raw. Then I wash my left hand. I sniff one of the white towels. It smells of starch and airing cupboard. Perfect. I blot my hands on the towel and then take off my clothes and pull on my pyjamas.

I brush my hair thirty-one times until it wobbles and crackles with static.

I haven't been to the loo for hours, so I push the door open, trying not to make a noise. There are only two other doors on this landing. I nudge one with my fingernail and sigh with relief when I see a bathroom.

I place some tissue on the rim and lower my bottom on to the toilet. My pee tinkles noisily into the bowl.

Now I'll have to wash my hands all over again.

By the time I've finished it's nearly quarter to eleven and I'm dizzy with tiredness.

But there's one more thing. I need to jump.

I try sitting still on the bed and seeing if the desire will go away if I ignore it.

It doesn't.

I can't go and jump on the stairs and risk waking everyone up.

I lay out one of the white towels on the floorboards.

Then I jump, as light as I can. One hundred and twenty-eight times on tiptoe, skin on fluffy cotton. By the time I've finished, the cotton feels like a cheese-grater on the soles of my tender feet.

I sniff the duvet, peel it back and slide in. My

tired bones shift about on the cool clean sheet.

'It'll be fine,' I say to myself. 'It's going to be OK here. Go to sleep.'

The birds begin some sort of mental dawn country chorus at three.

I lie awake for hours.

Chapter Six

I'm woken by the whine and clink of a milk van.

It's just gone six and I've had two hours' sleep.

I think about Fran, still asleep hundreds of miles away, her smooth brown cheek pressed into a pink pillowcase, her mother bustling around the kitchen, putting together packed lunches and schoolbooks, heating up porridge and scraping yellow butter across crusty brown toast.

I swallow hard, a mixture of hunger and fear. Fran will look for me as the school bus passes my house. What will she do when I don't come out? Will my stepmother tell her I've gone to the local hospital or will she make up some other excuse?

Fran will find me, I decide. She's not going to accept any old explanation. She'll find me and take me back to her house. I'll live with Fran and her mother until I hear from Dad. My stepmother won't want me back, so Fran will just have to take me in. I'll become part of that warm, bustling, normal family. They'll let me get on with my rituals and everything will work out fine and then Dad will take me home.

I slide my feet out of bed and into my slippers. I pad over to the sink. There's plenty of time to get my morning rituals done, but one little problem. No Green Day to time it to.

I look around the room. There's a portable CD player stashed underneath a small brown desk by the window, but no CDs with it.

I dig out my mobile phone and set it to 'choose ringer'. I select a tune called 'The

Entertainer'. It's a silly tune – Mum and Heather used to bash it out on our piano, giggling like mad after a glass of wine – but it'll do.

I set targets: sixteen repeats of the tune for washing my left hand, ten for my face and another sixteen for the right hand. Then another sixteen repeats for brushing my hair.

This works quite well, although the tinny little tune isn't a patch on Green Day.

I open my suitcase and rifle through my clothes, pull open the doors of a large pine wardrobe and hang things up with four centimetres in between each item.

I put on a plain white T-shirt and a pair of cut-off jeans. I do my jumps on the towel in bare feet and then slide into a pair of silver flip-flops and tie my hair into a short pony. I hook a pair of small dangly silver hearts through my earlobes. Not too long, not too short. Fran would say I'm in 'average' mood.

I survey the results in the mirror. Somebody has polished it to perfection. No smears and smudges. For once I can concentrate on how I look.

A girl with red-raw cheeks and fuzzy black hair stares back me. In her eyes is a look of uncertainty.

'You'll do, gorgeous girl,' whispers my mother's ghost.

My heart leaps with pleasure and relief. I need Mum with me today.

I perch on the bed and text Fran.

'Been sent to weird place in country,' I type in. 'Not sure when home. Miss u. Z.'

By the time I've opened my bedroom door and crept down the first flight of stairs, my confidence is fading fast.

All the bedroom doors on the landing below are shut. A faint snore rises and falls from beyond one of them. There's no sign of life, and no sign of breakfast. My stomach sucks itself in with a gurgle. My mouth is dry. I have a sour, sick feeling inside. The last thing I ate was the tuna sandwich in Heather's car.

I ease my way down another flight of stairs taking care not to touch the banisters.

When I reach the ground floor, I glimpse a black Aga in the room at the back of the house. I head for the kitchen, my flip-flops slapping on the tiled floor.

I stop short on the threshold.

Major Germ Alert.

I'm staring at a bright, square, roomy kitchen with a fireplace at one end and an Aga running along one wall, a set of sash windows along the other. There's obviously been some sort of massive party. In the middle sits a long wooden table strewn with dirty plates and cups. On the windowsill, egg cartons packed with green

58

sprouting things jostle and crowd for space. The tap is dripping into a sink full of pans with crusty brown stuff stuck on them. There's a faint smell of old omelette and stale beer. Chairs are dotted around the kitchen floor at random angles. Two bowls of stinking cat food flow over on to a fish-shaped mat. A radio babbles to itself in the corner. The floor is strewn with magazines, cushions, crisp packets and coats.

While I'm standing there taking all this in, a huge boiler whooshes and flares into life, nearly giving me a heart attack.

How am I going to eat any food that comes out of this kitchen?

How am I going to get *into* this kitchen to put the kettle on?

I run back down the hall and tug at the front-door catch.

Locked.

And, even if I did get out, I have no idea

where I am or how to get home from the country.

'Calm, Zelah,' I say. 'Deep breaths.'

Despite the horrendous mess in the kitchen, my stomach is still growling with hunger.

I tiptoe towards the sink, holding my arms rigid by my sides, trying not to brush against anything.

I fumble in my pocket for tissues, wrap one around each hand and pull open the cupboard underneath. Leaning against one another like hopeless drunks is a selection of Natural Earth cleaning products in green and orange bottles and a packet of new washing-up gloves.

'Thank you, thank you,' I whisper. My voice has dried to paper.

I roll up my sleeves, stretch the rubber gloves as high up my arms as possible, twiddle the radio knob until the familiar sound of Radio One invades the kitchen and get stuck in.

*

After one hour of spraying, scrubbing and tidying, my nose is running and my stomach is trying to eat itself but the room looks less like the aftermath of a riot and more like what it is: a homely, country kitchen with lots of pine shelves and flowery china.

I'm squirting germ-killer around the sink and giving it one last go with a metal scourer when my neck starts to prickle and turn cold.

I turn around.

A girl is leaning against the doorframe with her arms folded, chewing gum. The expression on her face is a mixture of patience, amusement and curiosity.

'I'd say you were the cleaner, only I know for a fact that we're still saddled with dear old Doris,' she says.

'So you must be the new girl. The Doc said you'd be here today. I'm Lib, by the way.'

I pull off my gloves, wipe my dripping nose

with a tissue wrapped around my right hand and then scrunch it up with my left before lobbing it into the bin. I wash my left hand, wrap another tissue around it and reach for the radio to turn down the volume.

"S all right,' says the girl. 'Leave it on. The Doc always tunes into some crap on Radio Three. This is better, but still a bit over-commercialised if you ask me.'

The Madonna song that Heather loves comes on. The girl groans and waves a squashed cigarette packet in my direction. I shake my head. She pulls one out with a grubby hand in a fingerless glove and sticks it into her mouth. Her bottom lip has a gold ring through it and there is a dark mole just above her top one, underneath her nose. Her hair is the sort of hair I pretend to hate but secretly admire: dyed yellow, short and peaked up on top with a serious amount of black root showing through.

The girl is big-boned with a large white face and a gappy grin. She's wearing pink pyjamas with a green parka slung over the top and fuzzy pink bed socks. The whole effect is bizarre, but somehow works.

I feel a prude in my boring jeans and neat T-shirt.

'Well?' she says. 'Gonna introduce yourself, then, or are you just gonna stand there flapping your rubber gloves at me?'

'Zelah,' I say. 'Zelah Green.'

The girl gives a snort of laughter.

'Sorry,' she says. 'It's just a bit more exotic than I was expecting. You don't look very exotic.'

From anyone else this would be an insult, but Lib manages to make it funny and I find myself smiling despite trying not to.

'What time's breakfast in this place?' I say. 'I'm starving.'

Lib laughs again. 'I wouldn't use that

63

expression around here,' she says. 'There's one person who might take offence.'

I haven't any idea what she's talking about, but I'm still smiling.

Lib is pulling eggs from the fridge and cracking them on the rim of a glass bowl.

'We do our own breakfast in the week,' she says. 'It's easier that way. Wouldn't be fair on the Doc to have to cook loads of different meals.'

'Why does everyone have a different meal?' I say.

She shoots me a look, raising her brown pierced eyebrows up towards her yellow fringe.

'You'll find out soon enough,' she says. 'But, as I'm in a good mood and you're new, I'll make you breakfast today. Just this once.'

The hiss of an egg hitting hot fat makes my stomach leap in anticipation.

'I like the yolks runny and the whites nice and crispy,' I say.

Lib splutters with amusement from where she's jiggling the frying pan around.

'If you carry on like that around here, they'll nickname you Princess,' she says.

I shrug.

Dad used to call me that when he was in a good mood. Compared to some of the names I've been called at school, it doesn't sound bad at all.

I have to run up to my room for a clean towel to put on the kitchen chair. Seats have had thousands of bottoms on them. Bottoms are well-known carriers of germs.

Lib watches me spread the towel over the scuffed wooden seat, but says nothing. She shovels food down with her elbows stuck out like bent branches and her mouth scrunched up, scowling with concentration.

Whilst I'm cutting into my second yolk with

a sigh of pleasure, another girl, younger than Lib and with long brown hair hiding half of her face, slopes into the kitchen, says, 'Oh hi,' in an offhand, disinterested way, grabs a yoghurt and disappears again.

'That,' says Lib, pushing her plate away and reaching for her fags again, 'was Alice. She's allergic to just about everything in the world. Oh, and she doesn't eat.'

'Except for yoghurt,' I say.

Lib is putting the eggs back into the fridge.

'Don't be fooled by that,' she says. 'The yoghurt will probably last her all day, if not all week.'

I'm silent for a moment, enjoying the post-egg hit of satisfaction and watching Lib as she pours a glass of water, gulps it down and then lights her fag.

She seems happy enough in my company, so I risk another question.

'What are you in here for?' I say.

Lib scrapes back her chair and stands up, still grinning.

'Me?' she says. 'Oh, there's nothing wrong with me. House clown, I am. Keep everyone laughing. I'll be out of here soon.'

She ambles towards the kitchen door, sucking hard on her cigarette, but then turns around.

'OCD, yeah?' she says.

My smile fades. I give a short, curt nod, trying not to take on the title as it whizzes across the kitchen towards me, looking for a home.

'We've had a few of those in here before,' says Lib. 'One left last week, in fact. She had your room. Anyway – catch you later. I need to buy fags before my session.'

She leaves me puzzling over 'session' and feeling deflated. They've had a few of me here before, then.

I'm not as unique as I thought.

I'm staring at the tabletop, picking off crumbs, lost in thought, when a man who looks like Jesus wanders into the kitchen, clutching his head and yawning.

'If we've run out of painkillers, I'm going to die,' he says.

He stops dead and stares about him.

'Is this the same kitchen I left last night?' he says. 'Only it looks like somebody's been in and waved a magic wand.'

I'm just plucking up courage to ask what his problem is and why he's the only adult in a houseful of crazy teenagers, when the man holds out his hand towards me.

'I'm Josh, by the way,' he says. A clutch of knotted leather bracelets slithers down his arm towards me.

'I own this place.'

Chapter Seven

I ignore the hand.

'Rituals,' I say, by way of explanation.

'Oh shit, of course,' says the man. He really does look like Jesus.

I sneak a peek at his feet. Yup – he's even wearing the battered brown sandals. He's got long, soft, mud-coloured hair and a wispy beard and he's got the same little round glasses as the Doc, except whereas her eyes are bright and awake and firm, his are sleepy and half shut and misty, as if he's thinking of something he loved and lost.

'I'm so sorry about the mess,' the man is

saying. 'Wednesday nights are always dodgy. I blame it on the chemicals in the Chinese takeaway.'

He delivers this line with a soft wink and a soppy grin.

'Do you want a coffee?' I say. To my horror, I'm blushing.

The man is already hunting around for jars and cups but at that he turns round and blesses me again with his disarming smile.

'This place will soon knock those manners out of you,' he says. 'Shame. I think you're great.'

My heart is doing flips and hops and missing beats. I'm going insane. One minute I'm laughing at this man in my head for being a nerdy Jesus-look-alike, the next he's a grinning Sex God and I'm feeling as if the legs on my chair are about to give way beneath me.

'Giving you the old patter, is he?'

The Doc's just come in. She touches the man

lightly on the shoulder and smiles at me.

'This, as he probably hasn't bothered to tell you, is my husband, Josh,' she says.

My heart falls to the ground and is kicked until it lies dead.

'Oh,' I say. 'Husband. Hello.'

'He has a way with the ladies,' says the Doc, peering with a frown at the green shoots growing on the windowsill. She is minus the apron today, but still wearing the white linen shirt and grey skirt. 'But the best thing is he's completely unaware of it.'

Josh is staring at her with a bemused look upon his saintly face.

'I'll leave you women to it,' he says. 'I've got a toilet to unblock and then I need to brave Caro's den.'

This is the second time I've heard the name 'Caro'. I remember the appalling scream from last night.

'She's in isolation today,' says the Doc, as if this explains everything. 'She's having a rough time at the moment. Josh is having a session with her later.'

'What do you mean?' I say. Is she talking about massage? Or yoga? Mum used to say that yoga was very calming to the soul. When I came home from school she was often to be found on a green mat with her legs knotted round her head. It never looked very calming to me. I tried it once and cricked a muscle in my neck.

The Doc is cradling her cup of coffee at the kitchen table.

'The kids here all have sessions,' she says. 'Either with Josh, or with me. We use behavioural therapy, which means we address patterns of behaviour and look at how we might break them.'

When she says 'break', I feel unsteady, as if somebody has pulled a rug from under my feet and replaced it with a barrowful of sharp, uneven rocks.

I grip the sides of my chair and hook my feet round the bar underneath.

'Your first session won't be until this evening,' she says. 'Until then you're free. Treat the place as home!'

She bustles out again, leaving me staring at my empty plate.

It's only eight o'clock in the morning. At home I'd be doing my rituals and getting ready for school about now.

Everything's been thrown upside down. All the usual time frames have been shattered. I can't even do my jumps on the top step in case somebody sees.

The kitchen is quiet and empty. A cat thunders through the cat-flap, gulps down a plate of Whiskas, sneezes and bolts outside again. I shudder. Cats carry a lot of germs.

Upstairs I can hear taps running, doors slamming and voices calling out to one another.

Fran, I think. *I'll go upstairs and see if Fran has replied to my text.* Or maybe Dad's tried to call me. That will kill, oh, about two minutes of this longest-ever morning. Then I can do my handwashing again and work out what to do next.

I creep upstairs. On the first floor, all the doors are open now except for the bathroom. I can hear the trickle of a bath being filled.

I try not to look inside each room as I pass by, but it's hard to resist.

In the first one is the girl who took the yoghurt – Alice, bending over, tying up her trainers. She's wearing dark-green baggy combats and a long-sleeved green top, even though it's boiling hot outside. Where her hair falls away from her neck I see blue veins bulging out and the jut of her collarbone.

In the room opposite there's a blue bed

made up as if nobody's slept in it. There's a poster of Pamela Anderson tacked to the wall over the bed. No signs of life.

The room adjacent to that one is about as messy as the kitchen was. There are books and CDs all over the floor and a bundle of rumpled clothes strewn across the bed. I recognise Lib's green parka and smile. It's a relief to see something familiar.

The room at the end of the corridor has the door shut and the sound of a hairdryer coming from it. As that's the room I heard snoring from last night, I reckon that this is Josh and the Doc's room.

I climb the narrow stairs to the floor where my little bedroom is.

As I get to the top I notice that the door next to the bathroom is open a fraction.

I peer through the crack, holding my breath.

There's a girl sitting in a window seat. Her

legs are bunched up underneath her and long wings of fair hair fall across her face, catching the sunlight.

The girl is busy doing something with her right hand.

I'm dazzled by the sun and struck by how pretty the girl is, a skinny blonde modern angel sitting in profile against an old sash window.

There are pictures pinned all over the walls of this attic room. Some are done in an angry red blaze of paint, others are sharp-edged cartoons in black and white. With a shock of envy, I realise that the girl has painted them herself.

She's doing some sort of painting right now.

I can't see what she's holding – her hand's obscured by one wing of hair dipping down across her arm, but she is taking great care over her work.

She's so into what she's doing that she hasn't noticed the stream of red paint dripping from her brush on to the pale floorboards.

I clear my throat. It's stressing me out to see the watery red falling on to the white floor.

The girl looks up, startled.

Her face is narrow and hostile, sickly grey with a light sheen of sweat on the forehead.

Something falls to the ground with a tinkle.

She pulls her sleeves down, too late.

The stuff dripping on to the floor is forming little red veins that trickle towards me.

It's not paint.

Chapter Eight

I only once saw so much blood coming out of a person.

On the day before Mum died I visited the hospital with Heather. We perched on the uncomfortable ridges of Mum's special mattress.

She wasn't talking much, but her eyes spoke volumes. They glowed and sparkled as I talked about what I'd done at school and what I was planning to do over the weekend.

'That's nice, love,' she said, when I'd finished going on.

Then she shot up in bed, coughed up a great lungful of dark blood all over my white skirt and fell back down like one of those cardboard people you shoot at a fairground.

Heather put her arm round me and led me out of the ward while the nurse cleaned Mum up.

The skirt already had a pattern of deep red flowers so Heather washed it in some special stuff for me and I carried on wearing it, but I never felt right in it after that.

The girl in the window seat is swearing and wrapping her long sleeves round her wrists.

I pull out a tissue and pass it to her. As she lifts her sleeve to apply it I catch a glimpse of her arm.

The skin is raised in bumps and ridges of angry red. All up her arm are criss-crossed lines, some weeping and sore, others healed and white.

'Get lost,' says the girl. 'You're not supposed

to be in here anyway.'

I bend down, wrap a tissue round my hand and pick up a metal nail file from the floor.

I hand it back to her.

'I didn't realise you could do such a lot of damage with a nail file,' I say. It sounds crass, but what else am I supposed to say?

I like what you've done to your arm.

Is it fun, hacking holes in your own skin?

You really should put a plaster on that.

The girl pulls her sleeves down again and slumps forward with her head on her knees.

'Do you want me to get someone?' I say.

She lifts her head up and regards me with cold eyes.

'You some kind of do-gooder?' she says. She's older than I first thought – fifteen or so. Her body is tiny, but there are worn blue shadows under her eyes.

'No,' I say. 'I've just got here. I'm in the room

next door.'

'Oh yeah, the OCD,' says the girl, disinterested. She turns away, gazes out of the window.

I feel a flash of anger.

'I have got a name, actually,' I say. 'Zelah Green.'

That gets her turning back round sharp.

'What kind of a weird name is that?' she says. 'Your mum got issues with you?'

'She's dead,' I say.

The silence is charged with several things. I can see the girl trying to backtrack, apologise even, but she's gone too far.

I feel sick at the mess on the floor. Embarrassed. Awkward.

There's only one thing to do.

I walk away.

'Yeah, catch you later, OCD,' she says. Her voice is loaded with disgust.

She puts on a Marilyn Manson CD as I shut the door to my own room. The savage roar of the music bursts through the wall and casts a black shadow of menace over my white furniture.

I rip my earrings out and chuck them back in the box. I have to scrub my hands sixty-two times each to get rid of the feeling of the blood.

I check my phone for a message from Fran. Nothing.

The Doc whacks an old gong in the hall to summon everyone down to lunch.

She's changed into a sleeveless orange summer dress with roman sandals and a gold ankle chain. Her curly grey hair is as wild as ever.

Josh is already in the kitchen in shorts and a white shirt, dishing up some sort of rice concoction and buttering soft brown rolls. He is mock-conducting an imaginary orchestra in between ladling the steamy, starchy risotto on to plates. Radio Three has won the battle of the airwaves again.

'Zelah, can you pour the drinks?' he says. He waves in the direction of three cartons of orange and apple juice.

The table is only laid for six.

'Sol's gone home for a day or two,' says the Doc, reading my mind as usual. 'He'll be back.'

'Not that you'd notice he's gone,' says Lib, twirling into the room and grabbing a bread roll from the basket Josh is putting on the table. 'He's a man of few words, our Sol. And that's an exaggeration.'

'Lib,' says the Doc with a reproving frown. 'You should let Zelah make her own mind up about people. And you shouldn't tease people who aren't around to defend themselves.'

'Ooh, sorry,' says Lib, but her plump features

are spread in a wide grin. She's wearing a hooded black sweatshirt and grey tracksuit bottoms. Her feet are still shoeless but her socks have changed from baby pink to fuzzy white. She's run some sort of hair gel through her peaky blonde fringe so that it stands to attention like a line of rigid white ferrets.

'Sit down, you lot,' says Josh. As he's putting mushroom risotto in front of us, Alice drifts into the kitchen with a sullen expression on her face. She sits down and hugs her own elbows, staring at the plate.

Her cheekbones cut through the pale skin underneath her eyes. There is a fine moustache of soft down on her upper lip and her teeth bulge out slightly. Her long brown hair is wispy and unwashed. Despite all this she's the prettiest person in the house. Except for maybe Josh.

'Now,' says the Doc, passing round a dish of

green broccoli with slivers of grey-yellow Parmesan on top. 'Have you two met Zelah?'

There are brief nods from Alice and Lib.

I don't mention my meeting with Caro earlier. Something tells me that the less I let on about what I saw, the easier my life at Forest Hill House will be.

The others begin to eat. Well – Lib does, shovelling rice into her mouth as if it's her last meal ever. Josh too eats with enthusiasm, grains of rice getting caught up in his beard and then dropping like tiny white maggots back on to the plate.

The Doc discards her knife and uses her fork to scoop up rice with her right hand, left elbow resting on the table.

I pull my own knife and fork out of my pocket and slide them into place. The Doc and Josh act as if they don't see.

Alice pushes her food around her plate and

from time to time, brings one fork prong to her lips where she pushes in a single grain of rice.

'Try a small bit,' says Josh, sliding the bread basket towards her.

Alice breaks open a wholegrain roll, refuses the butter and picks seeds off the top, placing them between her lips as if they might explode in her mouth.

Lib is rolling her eyes at me.

'You'll get used to this madhouse,' she says. 'Number one lunatic is upstairs. You've still got that pleasure to come.'

'Lib, shut up and get the pudding out of the oven,' says Josh.

Lib leaps up and returns with a blackberry crumble and a small yoghurt. She passes this to Alice.

Alice pushes back her chair, puts the yoghurt in the pocket of her baggy trousers and leaves the room with a murmur of thanks. At least, I think that's what it is. It sounds like 'ffa'.

'Believe it or not, she used to be worse than that,' says Lib.

I look at the plate Alice left behind her. Messed-around risotto lies in cold circular trails.

'Crumble?' says Josh.

I've brought my own spoon too. I pass my plate and let him pile it up with the steaming purple mess.

The Doc is waiting in one of the upstairs offices at half past five.

'Come in,' she says, smoothing down her orange dress and fixing me with her bright, assessing smile.

The room is painted in careful tones of grey and beige. There is a wooden desk by the window and a tall metal filing cabinet up against the wall.

The Doc is not sitting behind the desk but in

front of it in a black chair with a big circular back. She has slipped off her roman sandals and is rubbing one foot against the other on the rough grey carpet.

Dirt Alert.

This bothers me. All that crap she must be picking up on the soles of her feet.

She sees my look and puts her shoes back on again, sits up straight.

'Take a seat,' she says, gesturing towards a smaller version of her black chair.

I produce a sheet of A4 and lay it over the seat of the chair.

I see her noting all this as I sink on to the crackle of paper. She doesn't write it down, but you can see her brain computing it, storing the file away to be clicked upon and reopened later.

'OK,' she says. 'First session is about talking. I'm not going to make you do anything. We're just going to plan out your treatment.'

I twiddle with the frizzy ends of my hair. It feels like a matted scouring brush. I like the Doc, and all that, but I still don't really know what I'm doing in this place.

My eye alights upon a small dark smudge of something on the pale wall ahead. There are tissues in my pocket. I itch to get them out. I grit my teeth and sit on my hands.

The Doc is watching me with her head tipped to one side.

'If it makes you feel better, go and wipe it off,' she says.

I get up, go over to the wall, wipe off the offending smudge and wrap the dirty tissues in a clean one.

The Doc waits until I'm settled back on to my sheet of paper and then leans forward in her chair so that I can see all the tiny crinkles around her eyes.

'Zelah,' she says. 'Do you ever wish that you

could be free of your rituals?'

I consider this for a moment but it's like she's asking whether aliens are likely to land in a shopping centre and kit themselves out in TopShop. It's not something I've ever really thought about in any great detail. I mean – my rituals are just part of my life. They'll be there forever. Won't they?

'Not necessarily,' says The Doc.

I've said the last part out loud.

'If you want,' she says, 'we can work on ways together to get rid of them.'

I feel that great whooshing sense of panic again, like the floorboards have been pulled up under my feet, the ceiling is about to splinter into dust and plaster and I'm going to be sucked up through the open roof into a great, dark, hostile sky.

'Maybe I don't want to get rid of them,' I say. My voice has gone hoarse and my breath comes out in funny little jerks. I fold my arms tight across my chest in an effort to stop shaking.

I want to go and jump, thousands and thousands of good jumps, until I feel better. My body is itching to run to the stairs.

The Doc is still smiling. A flicker of anger passes through me. Why is she always smiling? Doesn't anything ever rile her? Like the fact that I'm shitting myself about being in therapy, for starters?

'I didn't ask to come here,' I manage, through tight lips. 'There's nothing wrong with me,' I add. 'Until I came here I coped with everything fine.'

The Doc is still nodding, smiling.

'Perhaps we'll draw this session to a close,' she says. 'I can see you've had enough.'

I'm standing up now.

'You're right there,' I say. It comes out as a bitter, hissing spit of anger. 'I've had enough of this place already. You and those screwed-up kids.'

I fling open the door until it bangs against the wall and leaves another black mark, but I'm past caring. For all I know, the Doc might have put the first smudge there on purpose. Testing me. Finding out how bad my 'little problem' really was. The only problem I really have is being stuck in this place. I have to get out.

I make a plan to contact Heather and ask her to come and get me.

I storm out of the office and run up the tiny flight of stairs to my attic room.

Then I lie face down on a towel on my bed and howl.

*

I must have fallen asleep because I wake up in a pile of warm dribble with a mouthful of wet cotton.

Someone is saying my name in a low voice.

'Mum?' I say, still half asleep.

I struggle into a sitting position. My head feels clogged and heavy, as if I've been asleep for hours.

At first I can't see anyone in the room.

She's sitting over by the door, her back up against it.

Caro.

Chapter Nine

'OCD, you can snore for England,' she says. Her sleeves are pulled down over her skinny wrists and her black eyeliner is more pronounced than ever.

'It's you,' I say. Stupid. Of course it's her. It couldn't really be anyone else, not with that foul mouth, blonde hair and grumpy expression.

Caro gets up.

She sits on the edge of my bed and looks down at her narrow fingers with their diamond-studded black nails and then into my hot, plump, red-cheeked face.

I'm wary of her, remembering what I saw

earlier. I need to wash my hands and face, but I don't want to do my rituals in front of this girl.

'So, OCD,' she says, 'why didn't you tell the Doc what you saw me doing?'

I shrug.

'Not my business,' I say. 'All I want to do is get out of this place.'

The girl laughs, a husky sound that turns into a smoker's cough.

'Yeah, right,' she says. 'Everyone says that. Nobody thinks that they've got anything wrong at all. Blah blah blah.'

I draw myself up until I am sitting, straight, rigid.

'I'm quite happy,' I say. 'I don't need to be here.'

Caro raises her dark eyebrows at me, amused.

'You've got serious issues, man,' she says.

That's rich, coming from a girl whose arms look like pink Shredded Wheat.

As she's being so blunt with me, I decide to be blunt back.

'Why were you screaming on the night I arrived?' I say.

Caro becomes very interested in picking out bits of dirt from behind her fingernails. *Dirt Alert*. I shift away from her, trying to track where it ends up.

'Josh took away my sketchbook,' she says. 'They're always encouraging me to express myself, but then they don't like what I draw. Can't win.'

'Can I see your sketches?' I say, surprising myself.

She fiddles with the frayed edges of her khaki top.

'Erm, maybe later,' she says. 'It's kind of personal.'

'OK,' I say. My tears have dried to a crispy fug on my cheeks.

'I designed these,' says Caro, holding out her fingernails for me to inspect.

We exchange miniscule smiles. Well, mine's a smile. Caro's is more like a cheek-twitch, as if she's shrugging off a persistent moth.

She stands up to leave.

'Can I ask a favour?' I say.

'Well, I suppose I owe you one for not telling the Doc about me,' she says. 'Shoot.'

'Could you keep the Marilyn Manson down a bit?'

Caro turns to me with a glower.

'Can't do that,' she says. 'Manson is my number one therapy.'

'Sounds like a mess to me,' I say.

'Naah,' says Caro.

She jumps up and heads for the door. She stops in the doorway and without turning round says, 'His lyrics are all about people who don't fit in.'

Two days later and there's still no word from Fran.

There's a new face at the supper table.

A boy is sitting opposite me, shovelling up spaghetti and gulping it down without lifting his head.

Josh is leaning back in his chair with a lazy smile on his features, sipping beer from a bottle. He always looks as if he's either just got out of bed or is longing to get back into it. I wonder if there's ever an hour in the day when his eyes open to their full capacity and he walks with purpose. I've only ever seen him slope about in his sandals, yawning and bestowing his kindly smile upon us.

The Doc is eating with her elbows propped up on the table and her gold bangles slithering down her brown arm. She has her beady eyes fixed upon the boy.

'Sol,' she says. 'This is Zelah. Say hello.'

Lib, sitting to my right, sniggers at this and becomes the victim of one of the Doc's frowns.

'Sorry,' she says. 'It's just, well, you know.'

I concentrate on winding strings of pasta round my fork. I wish that Caro was here but she's still confined to her room.

Sol lifts his head and gives me a brief glance and a nod. His eyes are unsmiling, dark brown with huge pupils. His head is shaved to a black shadow and his skin is about fifteen shades darker than my own pasty variety.

The Doc is refilling glasses with wine, beer and juice.

'Sol doesn't always feel like talking,' she says. 'But that's fine.'

'And Lib more than makes up for it,' says Alice, who is huddled over a small portion of food with her thin wings of hair dipping on to the table.

I'm still looking at Sol. He has the most beautiful face I've ever seen. I can't imagine now how I thought that Josh was so good-looking. Next to Sol he's just an old bearded guy in silly shorts.

'Omigod,' says Lib. 'I think our Princess has got a crush.'

I flush and become very interested in my empty plate.

'Don't tease,' says the Doc. She passes a small pot of yoghurt to Alice. Alice scrapes her chair back and glides out of the kitchen.

She slips the pot into the swing-bin on the way out.

Lib rolls her eyes and shakes her head.

Sol works his way through a bowl of chocolate ice cream without once looking up.

Josh yawns and runs his hands through his floppy brown hair.

'Do you want this on your own plate?' the

Doc asks me, dipping an ice-cream scoop into hot water and plunging it into the tub.

I nod.

My eyes have filled up with tears.

I'm stuck here with all these weirdos but I just want to go home.

If only I knew where 'home' actually was.

I check my phone about a hundred times, but there's still no message from Fran or Dad. I put it down on the drawers by my bed and walk over to the door. Then I walk back and check it again. I lie on the bed. I sit up and check it again. I switch it off and on just in case the battery's gone dead. I take the little orange card out of the back and snap it back in again, slide the phone cover back on.

Nothing.

I even go into voicemail just to check that I've set it up right.

My own pre-Forest-Hill-House voice chirps back at me.

'Hi, this is Zelah. Can't get to you at the moment as I'm probably out having A Life somewhere, but leave me a message and I might call you back.'

The message was recorded before Dad disappeared. He gave me the phone last birthday. Silver, tiny, with one of those display screens so you can see who's calling.

Fran's definitely got the number. She used to text me all the time, even when we were sitting next to each other at school. She'd text under the desk, her thumb moving demon-fast, her innocent face concentrating on what the teacher was saying.

I look at the phone lying quiet and dark by my bed.

'Fran, where are you?' I whisper.

The silence is huge.

I'm almost glad when Caro puts on her Marilyn Manson and the walls start to vibrate.

My rituals go on for ages that night.

They've not been that bad for a long time.

I figure that if I double the number of face and hand scrubs, Fran might text me.

I wrap a tissue round the taps and turn on the hot water, wait till it heats up to scalding.

I plunge my right hand under it and wash it sixty-two times, soaping and rinsing over and over. The pain makes me gasp and swear, but Caro's music does a good job of drowning that out.

I sniff my red-raw hand. Clean.

I put my left hand under the tap and wash it sixty-two times.

I check the fingernails for any last trace of dirt. Clean.

I stare at my puffy cheeks in the mirror.

'If I can scrub my face one hundred times in less than five minutes, Fran will ring,' I say.

I fill the sink and find my nailbrush. I rub the bristles into the soap until it looks as if it is coated in white cream.

I wait until the minute hand on my clock hits twelve.

I scrub my right cheek fifty times with my right hand.

Then I do my left cheek fifty times with my left hand.

I splosh the water up over my face until all the soap has gone.

Five minutes and three seconds. Damn.

Fran won't ring now.

I rinse the soap scum out of the sink and leave the hot tap running.

There's only one thing to do.

I unwrap another bar of soap.

*

It takes me ages to get comfortable in bed. My face and hands are so raw that I can't rest them on the sheet for more than a few seconds.

I end up lying on my back with my arms straight down beside my body and my hands placed palm upwards. From above I must look as if I'm lying in state like a carved marble soldier on a tomb in a big cathedral. All I need is a small dog lying at my feet and a suit of armour on my noble, war-ravaged body.

I erase the dog from this picture.

Dogs carry a lot of germs.

I'm woken by the sound of tapping on my bedroom door.

'Are you asleep, Zelah?' says the Doc. Fat chance. She says this in a loud theatrical whisper accompanied by the rustling of skirts, the jangling of bracelets and the continual creak of the floorboard she's standing on.

'Not any more,' I say. I reach for my bedside lamp and glance at my mobile. Still nothing.

'Sorry,' says the Doc. 'I just wanted to remind you that you're booked in for another therapy session after breakfast tomorrow.'

I'm wide awake now.

'Just a very small step in the right direction,' she says. 'We're going to pick one thing you feel compelled to do and we're going to apply some logic.'

Her tall frame moves in shadow back towards the light in the hallway outside.

'Night,' she says.

I lie awake for three hours with my palms and face throbbing.

Then I get out of bed, lay my towel on the floor and do one hundred and twenty-eight jumps as quietly as I can.

There's a thumping on the wall.

'OCD,' says Caro. 'Leave it out, man. It's

two o'clock in the bloody morning.'

I have to finish so I do the rest as fast as I can.

Then I crawl back on top of the sheets and beg my mobile phone to ring until daylight creeps back in.

Chapter Ten

C aro's back downstairs the next morning, stirring two tablets into a glass of water.

She grunts at me as I slide two slices of white bread into the toaster.

'Headache,' she says. 'Some idiot kept me up half the night by banging up and down on the floor.'

She's looking at my flushed skin and baggy eyes.

'Sorry,' I say. 'Just had to finish something off.'

Caro raises a spoonful of cornflakes to her mouth and then lets the contents slop back into the bowl again. She does this ten times.

'Is this how you eat, OCD?' she says. She's in one of her foul, grumpy, razor-sharp moods.

I feel a rush of anger and panic.

'Just ignore her, Princess,' says Lib. She's sitting at the table twiddling the dial on her iPod. 'Caro's the first to poke fun at everyone else, but she's the worst psycho in here.'

Caro gives an angelic smile. She picks up her glass of water, takes a dainty sip and with one savage movement chucks the rest over Lib's face.

'Oh dear, whoops,' she says. 'Clumsy old me.'

She gets up so violently that her chair tips over. She leaves it on the floor and slams out of the room.

'That's nothing,' says Lib, checking her iPod for damage. 'She cut off my hair in the night once.'

'And smashed a glass coffee table with her fist,' says Alice. As usual her hair covers half her face. She's taking tiny nibbles round the edge of a cracker with the faintest smear of Marmite across it.

I scrape my own knife over the toast and sit down.

'Why is she so cross all the time?' I say. 'What happened to her before she came here?'

The girls exchange glances.

'We're not supposed to say,' says Lib. 'The Doc's always banging on about patient confidentiality.'

I nod. I'd rather they didn't find out about Mum and the cancer, or Dad leaving, or my difficult relationship with my stepmother.

We've all got secrets in this place.

'Great morning,' says Josh, ambling in with the milk. 'Makes you glad to be alive, doesn't it?'

'Yuk,' says Lib. She's grinning.

From two floors up the rumble of Marilyn Manson starts again.

*

My session with the Doc takes place up in my own bedroom. As we pass Caro's door I see her framed in that window seat again, head bent over her sketchbook.

'You let her have it back, then,' I say.

'Only thing that keeps her quiet,' says the Doc. 'Despite our doubts as to the subject matter, there's no denying that she's very talented. Seen any yet?'

'She won't let me.'

'She will do at some point,' says the Doc. 'Caro never does anything until she's ready. I think she likes you, actually. You might do her some good.'

'If liking somebody means growling at them and taking the piss, then yes, she must like me a lot,' I say.

The Doc laughs. Her eyes sparkle and crinkle up in the corners.

Maybe this session won't be too bad after all.

*

The Doc pulls back my curtains and lets sunlight flood over the floorboards. She takes a chair from the dressing table and sits in the middle of the room.

'You can sit on the bed, as we're being informal today,' she says.

I curl up on the duvet and lean back against the wall in a position where I can see the Doc and the display screen of my mobile phone.

'One thing,' she says. 'Do you mind putting that in your drawer, just for the session? I want your full attention.'

I wasn't expecting that. I tense up. What if Fran chooses that very moment to call? Will I hear the ringer from inside the drawer? Is my voicemail working properly so that she can leave a message?

My face is going through a variety of worried expressions, judging by the Doc's reaction.

'OK, compromise,' she says. 'Pass it here and

I'll put it in my pocket. I'll feel if there's a ring. Then I'll give it back to you. Promise.'

I snap the phone back into its plastic cover so that the Doc can handle it without making fingerprints. It disappears into the deep white pockets of her linen shirt.

'Now,' she says. 'First thing to say to you is that OCD is an illness. It is not you. It is not soul-of-Zelah. It's a separate thing.'

I chew on this one for a moment. It certainly feels like me. I try to imagine life without my rituals and I feel so dizzy that I bang my head against the wall and the bed threatens to shoot out from under me and leave me sprawled on the floor. What was I like before the rituals came into my life?

All I can remember is Mum. We hugged, lots. We held hands and went to the park. Hands seem to figure a lot in my memories of those days. Cool hands on my damp forehead when I was sick. Proud hands clapping in the air after the school play, so fast that I could see more than one pair at a time. The black opal ring on her fourth finger moving over my homework as she helped me, her dark head bent close to mine in the lamplight. Hands bathing me and rubbing shampoo into little lathery peaks on my head, holding out the soft towel for me to step into. Hands that were busy, plucking items from supermarket shelves and handing crisp bank notes to cashiers, bundling goods into plastic bags faster than they were being scanned in, pressing the beeper on the car key to unlock the doors. Capable hands, driving me home to tea and bed.

Holding Mum's thin hand in the hospital when she was dying.

'You miss her a lot, don't you?' says the Doc, doing one of her spooky mind-reading things.

I can't speak. I'm looking at my hands and

wondering how long it is since I let somebody hold them. Over two years, I reckon. Only Fran has been allowed to get close. And now where is she?

I swallow, looking at the outline of my phone in the Doc's white pocket. I'm expecting it to ring. People always ring at the most inconvenient times.

'I think,' says the Doc, 'that you developed your OCD after your mother died as a way of staying in control of your feelings.'

She's flicking through a folder as she says this. I recognise it as the one Heather passed to her on the doorstep when I arrived.

I shift on the bed, feeling hemmed in against the white wall behind me.

'Tell me how you feel if you miss any of your rituals,' she says.

That's easier.

'Sick,' I say. 'Panicky. Weird. Like the whole

115

day's sort of gone out of time.'

'What might happen if you don't do them?' she asks. 'For instance – if you didn't do your jumping tonight, what do you think would happen to other people?'

I wonder if this is a trap. If she's going to try to stop me jumping, I'm leaving this house. I don't care where I go. I'll run down the motorway and hitchhike all the way to Heather's house. She'll understand. She'll take me in.

'If I don't do it, it feels like someone I love will probably die,' I say. 'Mum died. Maybe if I'd had my rituals then, things would have turned out differently.'

The Doc is nodding, her gaze frank and warm.

'I can tell you something, God's honest truth,' she says. 'Nothing can stop the spread of that type of cancer. Your mother was very unlucky. It wasn't your fault.'

I don't believe this for a second, but I give

her what she wants, a brief nod and smile. I want my phone back. I want to get on with my washing. I need to rearrange my wardrobe to stop my things touching.

'We're going to do one small exercise right now,' says the Doc. 'Just to show you that nothing bad is going to happen to you if you come into contact with a bit of dirt.'

She glances over towards my sink.

In a flash I understand.

Major Germ Alert!

My breath starts to come in short gasps and my heart is pounding.

'I – can't,' I start.

The Doc goes to the sink and places her hand on one of the taps.

'I'll go first,' she says. She keeps her hand there for a few seconds and then removes it.

'Nothing bad is going to happen to me for doing that,' she says. 'Josh is still speaking to

Caro. The cat is still lying in the vegetable patch. My Aunt Maureen will be pottering around her garden in Brighton with a pair of shears and she won't have stabbed herself to death with them. More's the pity.'

I'm keeping a wary eye on what she's doing with the contaminated hand, but I snigger at the last part.

'Your turn,' says the Doc. 'I want you to touch one of the taps. Whichever one you prefer. For about two seconds. Then I want you to resist washing it for a whole minute. I'm going to time you.'

I get off the bed. The air in the room seems to have expanded. I am standing in the middle of an enormous empty space with nothing to hold on to. The tap looms, large, an occasional drip falling in slow motion into the white enamel.

'Go on,' says the Doc. 'I promise you that

nothing bad will happen. And I don't lie. Well – only about my age.'

I can't believe I'm even considering doing this.

'Can I put a tissue round part of the tap?' I say. I'm standing by the sink now, about half a metre away from touching it.

'No need,' says the Doc. 'It won't bite you.'

I take a deep shaking breath and extend one of my red fingers towards the cold metal. I've forgotten what it feels like to touch something someone else has just touched without the padding of a soft white tissue in between.

'Hold it for two seconds,' says the Doc.

I gasp as my finger brushes the chrome.

'One,' counts the Doc.

My whole body has gone into spasm. Tears stream down my face.

I screw up my eyes. I use every bit of strength to keep my finger in place. I can feel the germs penetrating into the fibres of my skin and flooding through my body.

'I want to stop,' I spit out through clenched teeth.

'Two,' she says. 'You did it!'

My legs give way. I collapse backwards on to the bed, holding my finger out in front of me so as not to touch anything else with it.

'That was the longest two seconds ever in the history of time,' I say.

'No, it was just two seconds,' smiles the Doc.

I need to wash, and fast. I can see the germs, evil, black and grinning at me from my frightened fingertip.

'No washing for one minute, starting from – now,' she says, frowning at her wristwatch.

I hold the finger as far away from my body as possible and grip that arm with my other one to stop the shaking.

'Thirty seconds to go,' says the Doc. I swear

she's counting seconds in minutes today.

'Twenty,' she says.

I'm holding my breath now to avoid breathing in the germs.

My lungs ache. My eyes water and I can feel myself going puce.

'Five,' says the Doc. 'Four – three – two – one – wash if you want to.'

If I want to?

I'm at the sink faster than you can say 'dirt'. Nothing has ever felt so good as that cascade of warm water running over my dirty finger. I lather it up with plenty of soap and do thirty-one quick washes. I'm aware that all the time I'm doing this, the Doc is observing me and scribbling notes in her book, but I'm past caring.

When I've finished washing, I dry off my hands on a clean towel and sit back down on the bed.

The Doc snaps her book shut and removes her round spectacles.

'Well done. You did it,' she says. 'I know that touching a tap is one small step for mankind but a huge step for Zelah Green. I'm impressed.'

'You're not going to make me do anything else, are you?' I say. The blood has drained out of my body. I want to curl up and hibernate.

She laughs and pops my mobile phone back on to the chest of drawers.

'Goodness, no,' she says. 'That's enough for the first session. I'm going to put you on some medication as well, and we'll arrange the next session for early next week.'

She closes the door behind her, leaving a scent of starch and dried roses in the air.

It's only lunchtime, but I'm shattered.

I check my mobile phone and lie down on the bed, intending to rest for a bit and then go down to lunch.

I fall asleep in about five seconds flat.

When I wake up, the afternoon is losing light and I've slept right through the lunch gong. The Doc or someone has been up with a tray and put it round the door. There's a plate of ham and mustard sandwiches and a glass of cranberry juice, along with a tiny white envelope.

Inside is a hand-drawn card with a cartoon of a black-haired girl with big scared eyes reaching out towards a giant-sized tap with an evil mouth full of spiky metal teeth.

It's clever. I laugh out loud. Caro.

The message in the card says, 'Well done for taking the first step,' and everyone has signed it. Lib's name is big and brash and followed by an exclamation mark. Alice has signed hers in a tiny spider scrawl. Caro has drawn a face with crossed eyes inside the 'o' of her name. Sol has just written 'Sol'. Josh and Erin have squeezed their names into the tiny amount of space left at the bottom.

I bite into the sandwich and enjoy the tang of the yellow mustard against the pale smoothness of the ham.

I sit on the bed and hug my knees and gaze at the card.

I did it, I think. I touched something for two seconds without a tissue. And nothing bad happened.

I finish my lunch and lie on the bed listening to the growl and howl of Marilyn Manson's voice through the wall. I'm getting used to it.

This afternoon would be a good one.

If only Fran would ring.

Maybe tomorrow.

Chapter Eleven

The radio's on in the kitchen and Alice is standing over a brown pottery bowl, beating something to death.

'Morning,' she says. 'Caro's birthday.'

I'm nearing the end of my second week at Forest Hill House and getting used to the routine. Alice and Lib are the first ones down for breakfast so that they can chat without Caro's sarcastic comments. Sol slopes in half an hour later. And Caro has to be dragged out of her bed with huge dark circles under her eyes.

Alice is waving something in my direction. Her thin arm holds out a wooden spoon dripping with cake mix. The arm trembles with the strain of holding it up long enough for me to clap my mouth round the mix without touching the wood of the spoon.

'It's gorgeous,' I say. Alice flushes with embarrassment and disappears under her hair to carry on beating.

'I wish someone had told me,' I say. 'I haven't even got her a card.'

Alice slops the cake mix from her bowl into a round tin and observes me from behind her right-hand wing of hair.

'Maybe the Doc thought you had more important things to worry about,' she says. 'But actually I'm rubbish at icing, so maybe that could be your present to Caro?'

I leap up, turn the radio up to full blast, and hunt around in the kitchen drawer for nozzles and syringes.

By the time Caro staggers in, rubbing her

eyes and complaining at the racket, a sticky, uneven chocolate cake sits in the middle of the kitchen table.

Caro holds the plate up to the light and inspects the lumpy layers and amateur icing.

'Random, or what!' she says. The smile fades from Alice's face. I flash my eyes at Caro and tilt my head towards Alice.

Caro gets it. She puts the cake down.

'Thanks, Alice,' she says. 'Sorry. I thought that OCD here had made it. In which case she'd still have been counting out the ingredients.'

I ignore the barb and wrap a tissue round the handle of the bread knife.

'Breakfast cake, anyone?' I say.

Caro gets a good selection of presents. The Doc and Josh have bought her an art kit, complete with brushes, watercolour pads and paint and little tubes of colour.

She scowls.

'I thought you didn't want me to paint,' she says.

'Caro, you've got a great talent,' says the Doc. 'It's just you don't always know where to draw the line. Oh blast.'

Caro smirks at the pun.

Lib hands Caro a small square parcel. Inside is a new Slipknot CD.

'Great,' I say. 'So I'll have to listen to that one through the wall now. Nice one, Lib.'

Sol hands over his parcel in silence. Inside is a folded square of black material. It opens out into a Marilyn Manson T-shirt.

'Oh, man,' says Caro, ripping off her green T-shirt and replacing it with the deathly white face of Marilyn.

'Cheers, Sol,' she says.

He looks at his hands, unsmiling.

Caro opens a few cards as Josh sets about

scrambling eggs for her birthday breakfast.

'Did you get one from your parents?' I say.

Everything seems to grind to a halt.

Josh's spoon stops stirring the eggs and freezes in mid-air.

The Doc pauses by the cupboard with a half-open tin of cat food in her hand.

Sol keeps his head bowed, but I catch him swapping looks with Lib.

Lib pushes her hands over her face and peeks out from between her fingers.

Alice vanishes behind her hair.

The only sound is that of the cat sneezing in tiny hiccups, over and over.

'Hairball alert,' says Lib. She shoos the cat out of its flap and into the garden.

With the tension broken, everyone resumes what he or she was doing with renewed vigour except Caro. She has stopped opening cards and is looking at me. A straight, defiant, challenging sort of look, chin lifted, eyes flashing.

'Caro, you don't have to . . .' begins the Doc.

'No, it's OK,' says Caro. 'Zelah wasn't to know.'

'Know what?' I say.

Caro sticks her finger into the chocolate butter icing on the cake and sucks it off.

'I don't live with my parents,' she says. 'They weren't the best role models in the world. And I think I'll shut up about it now, if you don't mind.'

She cuts herself a massive piece of cake and eats it, even though Josh is spooning yellow egg on to her plate at the same time.

'Alice is the only one who lives with both parents,' says Lib. 'I'm with my grandparents. Sol lives with his dad. What about you, Zelah?'

It's the first time I've been asked. With all eyes on me I can't be bothered to hide the truth.

'Dad's disappeared,' I say. 'My best friend hasn't contacted me once since I got here. Oh, and Mum's dead.'

Sol, who's been fiddling with a penknife up to that point, gives me a penetrating glare. I feel the Doc's hand hovering about ten centimetres over my shoulder as she passes by to make more tea.

'And I live with foster parents,' says Caro. 'And they're such super-duper posh gits with their petrol-guzzling people-carrier, ruining the environment. And I'm supposed to feel lucky to have them. Except I don't. And now this birthday stinks, just like all the others.'

With one quick gesture she brings her fist down into the cake left on her plate.

Sponge, chocolate buttons and icing pulp into a flat, squishy mess.

'Caro!' says the Doc. 'Alice spent ages on that cake. Apologise.'

'I hate chocolate cake anyway,' says Caro, flashing her evil smile. 'Ironic, isn't it? An anorexic making a cake. Bit like me slicing it up, I suppose.'

Josh has sunk further into his chair, shaking his head with a sad expression on his face. Scrambled egg is congealing into orange lumps on the plates in front of us.

'Get upstairs,' says the Doc. 'And let everybody else enjoy their breakfast.'

'Don't worry, I'm going,' says Caro. 'Bunch of losers.'

She pulls the Manson T-shirt off and shoves it back at Sol on her way past.

He gives a growl of frustration and slams out of the kitchen.

'Just another day of peace and love at Forest Hill,' says Lib.

Alice is trying not to cry so we all eat cake instead of scrambled egg and make a great play of enjoying it. Except for Alice. She pushes a sliver of sponge around her plate and brushes a single crumb on to her lip from the side of a fork prong.

'Honestly, she's a little devil, that Caro,' says the Doc. 'Did you see the look on Sol's face? He saved up to buy her that T-shirt.'

'It's my fault,' I say. 'I mentioned her parents.'

Lib laughs.

'Yeah, and if you hadn't said that, she'd have still blown up at something else,' she says. 'We've all got issues in here, but Caro likes to be a drama queen.'

I wonder what Lib's issues are. Ever since I arrived last week she's been friendly and upbeat. I don't want to risk upsetting anyone else so I keep quiet.

I've got worries of my own, anyway.

Therapy at eleven.

*

I leave the breakfast table before the Doc so I can do one hundred and twenty-eight jumps on the top stair without her seeing.

The plan backfires. Sol comes out of his bedroom in a black bomber jacket and stares at me.

Flirt Alert. That's a new one.

'Erm, sorry,' I say, squeezing up against the wall so that he can get past. Sol slips by. He's thinner than I thought, and shorter than all the girls in here. All the power is in his dark eyes and scowling expression.

As Sol edges past me I get a whiff of shower gel and tobacco.

He runs downstairs without looking back.

'Get a grip,' I say to myself. My cheeks are hot. 'He's just a boy. And he doesn't even talk.'

I start my jumps again from the beginning because once they're interrupted it doesn't count, but little images of Sol's olive skin and soulful brown eyes keep flashing up and interfering with my counting.

In my head Sol's grinning at me, one of his rare grins, and closing in on me, all the while pinning me to the wall with those amazing eyes.

I'm being all girly and shy and flirtatious, flicking my hair about and chewing the ends of it.

In the end I have to start all over again three times before I get to the end. The tender soles of my feet rasp against the hard insides of my trainers and I'm out of breath.

I haul myself upstairs by placing a tissue in my hand so that I can touch the banisters.

As I pass Caro's room I can hear Josh's gentle low murmur interspersed with Caro's high-pitched, indignant rant.

The door is shut, but outside in the attic hallway are shreds of cream-coloured paper and tiny red paintbrushes snapped in two. The wooden box lies like an upturned storm-tossed boat outside my room.

I wrap a tissue round my right hand, pick up all the brushes and bits of paper and put them back in the box; snap the lid shut and put it outside Caro's room.

Then I head for the sink to scrub the sourness of the morning off my face and hands.

The Doc is waiting for me in the therapy room.

There are no sinks in here, nothing except the pale carpets and wooden furniture.

I relax. Maybe we're just going to chat today.

'What a morning,' says the Doc. 'Not the happiest birthday we've had in this place.'

As if to illustrate her point there's a shriek of rage and a muffled slam from upstairs.

The Doc gives me a rueful smile.

'I think you're settling in well, Zelah,' she

says. 'The others certainly seem to have taken a shine to you.'

'Except for Caro,' I say. 'She hates everyone.'

I think of the morning when I saw blood dripping down from her wrists, and shudder.

'Caro isn't as angry as you all think,' says the Doc. 'Anyway – let's get back to you. How did you feel after touching the taps last week?'

'Tired,' I say. 'Shocked.'

'Anything bad happen as a result?' says the Doc.

I consider this for a moment in silence. Fran still hasn't rung me. Maybe she was just about to ring when I touched the taps and screwed up my usual routine. That could be the bad thing.

The Doc is waiting for me to reply. I like the way the sun picks up copper highlights in her hair and makes her white shirt look even whiter. I like her little round spectacles and kind bright eyes. I can trust her today, I think.

'My best friend hasn't called since I got here,' I say. 'Maybe when I touched the taps I put a jinx on her ringing me.'

'Or maybe,' says the Doc, twinkling at me, 'she's just been busy, or she's lost her phone, or she's writing you a long letter instead.'

This is a revelation. My feet feel as if they are unbolted from the floor. I'm flying around the room for a moment.

Fran could be OK.

And, if Fran's OK, then just maybe . . .

Dad's OK as well.

The Doc tells me we're going to use a numbers technique today. She's going to make me do something I don't want to do and I'm going to tell her how it makes me feel, out of ten.

'Follow me,' she says.

I traipse down the corridor to the bedroom she shares with Josh.

Uh-oh. Bedroom has en suite bathroom. *Germ Alert.*

'Sit,' she says, gesturing at her bed. It's made up to perfection: crisp antique linen pillows plumped like giant ravioli, white cotton sheets folded back over soft pastel-coloured blankets. By her side of the bed is a stack of books with frightening titles like *Discovering the Lost Child Within Your Troubled Teenager*, and *A Select Bibliography of Compendiums Relating to Mental Health Issues*. There are similar books on Josh's side of the bed, but he has some extra titles like *How to Destroy Slugs Using Organic Processes*, and *Eat Yourself Green: A Guide to Self-Sufficiency.*

'Tell me how stressed you are feeling right now, out of ten,' says the Doc.

My heart is racing at the thought of what might happen in the bathroom.

'Eight?' I venture.

She pushes open the bathroom door with

her foot, allowing me a glimpse of polished floor tiles and gleaming chrome. Her ankle bracelet jingles tiny silver bells.

'And now?'

'Nine,' I say.

The Doc writes this down.

Then she beckons me inside the bathroom until I am standing inside the doorway. We are facing the toilet.

The Doc points into the bowl.

'It's very clean,' she says. 'Doris gives it a ruthless scrubbing with disinfectant and she's been in this morning.'

I get it, quick as that. We're not doing taps today. We've moved on to Second Base.

'I'm not touching that,' I say. 'Forget it. No way.'

The bowl in front of me has stopped being a normal toilet and has morphed into a great gaping chasm of enamel mouth, as big as the caves I used to hide in when Mum took me on the beach in Cornwall. A faint gurgle comes from deep within the pipes. I swear I can see a hair floating on the surface.

'Out of ten?' says the Doc.

'Eleven,' I say. 'Twelve, thirteen, fourteen, fifteen, a thousand.'

I've backed away towards the sanctity of the bedroom.

'Zelah,' says the Doc. 'I'm going to go first. Bear in mind that I like to be clean and tidy too. Watch what I do.'

In front of my horrified gaze, the Doc plunges her hand inside the toilet and gives the inside a fond pat, just as she did to the cat after breakfast.

She holds the hand out towards me.

'Wash it,' I say. 'You've got to wash it straight away.'

'No, I don't,' she says. 'I can stay like this all

day if I want to. Because nothing bad is going to happen to me just because I touched a toilet.'

I breathe great slow breaths, trying to calm myself down.

'Phoo, phoo,' I go, hand on my chest, steadying my racing heart.

'That's it, good girl,' says the Doc. 'Right, your turn.'

She steps back to allow me to approach the bowl.

I'm so stressed that a weird Olympic-style commentary starts up in my head.

And here we have Zelah Green, the fourteen-year-old champion of rituals, attempting the afternoon toilet-touching event for the first time . . .

I take my first faltering step towards the rim.

And she's approaching the target, booms the voice. *Steady approach, good footwork . . .*

My right hand, naked and trembling, is now hovering over the inside of the toilet.

Will she set a new world record? screams the voice. *Will Zelah Green take the gold medal for bravery and/or total stupidity?*

'I'm going in!' I say.

I skim the curved cool surface of the bowl with the fingertips of my right hand and jump back as if I've been electrified.

And she's done it! shrieks the commentator. *Zelah Green wins the gold medal for toilet touching!*

Next thing I know I'm sprawled on the cold bathroom floor retching and gagging and the Doc is trying to help me up without handling me.

'Good girl, good girl,' she says. 'No, don't do that,' as she sees me heading towards the sink with a purposeful glint in my eye.

Me, the Doc and my soiled hand go back into the bedroom.

'Out of ten now?' she asks.

'Ten,' I say, straight away. This is without

doubt the most stressful thing I've ever done in my life.

The Doc ferrets around in her bedside drawer and comes up with a squashy pack of organic chewing gum.

'Want one?' she says, offering the green tube.

I reach towards it with my left hand. She shakes her head.

'I want you to take it with the right hand,' she says.

'But that's the – oh, crap,' I say. Of course she wants me to take it with the contaminated hand.

I take a sliver of wrapped gum from the packet and drop it like a hot potato.

'Pick it up and unwrap it,' commands the Doc.

She's got to be kidding, right?

'My stress level is now off the scale,' I say, but I pick up the piece of gum, unwrap it with my dirty right hand and hold the greying strip up for her inspection. I can't believe I'm doing all this, but I am.

'Do you like chewing gum?' says the Doc.

'No,' I say. I think of all the horrid cold hard lumps of masticated gum stuck underneath my desk at school and how I would try not to let the underside of the desk touch my school skirt.

'That's a shame,' she says. 'Because I want you to put that gum in your mouth and chew it for ten seconds, please.'

What???

I've touched the revolting gum with my horrid germ-infested finger and now she wants me to put the whole death-inducing combination inside my nice mint-fresh mouth where it will seep into the sanitised temple that is my body and cause undue havoc and destruction.

The Doc pops a stick of gum on to her own tongue, using her unwashed hand, and chews with her mouth open whilst staring me straight in the eye. The stick-stick noise of her chewing reminds me of the boys at school.

I fight it, but I feel a giggle coming on.

She winks and carries on. *Stick-stick-stick.*

'Oh, what the heck,' I say.

I shove the mint stick in, close my eyes and chew as hard as I can. The Doc counts down from ten seconds to one. I'm sure I can taste the germs.

'You're done,' she says.

I projectile-spit the gum out into her bin and run to the bathroom where I wash my hands thirty-one times on each side and rinse my mouth out until my teeth ache.

When I come out, we go back to the office and sit down. She says, 'Stress levels, out of ten?'

The strange thing is, I don't feel all that bad. Shaky, yes, but not as sick as I thought I would be.

'Six,' I say. 'And a half.'

'Good,' says the Doc. 'And remember – nothing bad will happen because of what you just did.'

I nod.

A faint glimmer of hope is trying to push through the big grey fug of fears and rituals.

Just as I'm getting up to leave, there's a tap on the door.

'Sorry to interrupt,' says Josh. 'There's a visitor for you, Zelah.'

Before I have a chance to ask who it is, he gestures someone through into the room.

Someone in high-heeled spiky boots, wearing a red leather jacket with sunglasses perched on her highlighted hair and a big soppy grin.

'Heather!'

'Got a surprise for you, kiddo,' she says.

Heather steps aside. Another, smaller person steps into the room and beams at me, a freckle-faced person with brown plaits wearing a pink sundress and a neat denim jacket.

Fran!

Chapter Twelve

The Doc, Josh and Heather do this really obvious thing of winking and gesturing and shuffling out of the office, closing the door behind them.

Fran and I are left facing one another.

I'm grinning so hard that my mouth feels bigger than my face.

'You're alive, then,' I say. Stupid comment but it's the only thing that comes into my head.

Fran. My best friend, standing in the middle of the office in her pale pink dress and denim jacket. I look at her shiny plaits and snub nose. She's even cleaner and neater than I remembered. Her flip-flops match the darker pink flowers on the dress and her toenails are done to perfection in scarlet.

'Let's go to my room,' I say.

We head upstairs. Lib's door is shut and I can hear the Arctic Monkeys and the whine of a hairdryer.

Sol's back, sitting on the edge of his bed and muttering into a mobile. He looks up with a glare as we go by and then does a double take as he sees Fran tripping along behind me like a small, glossy pony.

Something in me shrugs, sighs and withers.

I forgot that when Fran is about, I become invisible.

We sit on the bed, not touching of course, but close. She's bought me a bag of unnatural-looking pink shiny apples.

'I'm not ill,' I say. 'But cheers anyway.' I run

an apple under the tap, even though I hate their nasty cold hardness.

Fran observes her small feet in their pretty shoes, tipping up the toes towards her body with a critical frown and then releasing them.

I can see her trying to summon up the energy to speak over the crash of Caro's music. The volume's up louder than usual. I wonder if Caro has seen Fran come in and is doing this on purpose.

'Sorry,' I say. 'You don't notice it after a while. Like seagulls in Cornwall.'

Fran looks doubtful. Her family go on holiday to exotic castles in Europe.

'Doesn't it give you a headache?' she says.

I try to explain about the lyrics and how they mean something to a person like Caro. I talk about music being a release and a therapy and an expression of how a person is feeling, but I can see her glazing over and allowing her eyes to wander around my room, the bare walls, the white floor and the tiny bookcase.

'So,' I say, to get her attention back. 'How come you didn't reply to any of my texts for nearly two weeks?'

Fran is now fiddling with the pink cancer wristband she's wearing. I wonder if she put the band on because of my mum. A nasty little voice in my head says, *She probably just likes the colour.*

'Mum told me not to text you,' she mumbles.

Her mum?

'I thought she understood my, erm, problem,' I say. I still hate using the proper name for it.

'Yeah, she just thought we should let you get on with the treatment,' says Fran. She's shifting on the bed and avoiding my eye.

'Does my stepmother know where I am?' I say.

Fran looks even more uncomfortable.

'Well, erm, the apples are from her, actually,' she says.

As she says this I'm taking a bite. I spit out the mouthful of pink flesh into a tissue and chuck it in the bin. My stepmother has probably injected each apple with a syringe packed with dirt, just to spite me. Now I come to think of it, the apples do look a bit too perfect.

Through the wall Marilyn Manson is singing low and menacing, something about a long road out of hell.

Just as I'm wondering what on earth to say to my best friend's admission that she got all my texts and ignored them, or that my stepmother knows where I am and may turn up at any time, the door bursts open and Lib's untidy figure flies in, green Parka slung over one arm and blonde hair sticking up with new red tips. Behind her hovers Alice, dressed as usual in baggy jumper and shapeless trousers, despite the sunny weather.

Lib stops dead when she sees I have company.

'Oh,' she says. 'Sorry – me and Alice are going into town and we wondered if you wanted to come?'

I glance at Fran. She's looking at Lib's green combats, black sleeveless vest and baseball boots with something bordering upon disgust.

If Lib had asked me to go shopping this time last week, I'd have shuddered in horror and made some excuse to get out of it.

I look at her wide, friendly face and inhale the earthy smell of fags, canvas shoes and soap.

My body wants to leap up, grab a jacket and follow Lib and Alice to the shopping precinct.

My mouth does the polite, sensible thing.

'Fran's come a long way to visit,' I say. 'So I'd better stay in. But thanks for asking.'

Lib laughs her great guffaw.

'Princess, your manners are perfect,' she says. 'You've been well dragged up, I'll give you that.'

'My mum was strict about manners,' I say, surprising myself. Since she died, I haven't spoken about Mum without being prompted.

Lib starts to shut the door.

'Your mum sounds all right,' she says. 'Better than the binge-drinking waste of space that I grew up with.'

The door clicks behind her.

A few minutes later I see them, arm in arm, walking down the front path outside, doing a silly dance because they're excited that The Doc has allowed them a day out.

Something inside me flips with pain.

I turn back to Fran.

'How's school?' I say, even though I don't really care.

'Yeah, it's fine, but we've got a trip to France coming up and I so don't want to go,' says Fran.

'We've got to share a coach with Bradford Boys' School. Can you imagine?'

I can imagine. I can see it clear as anything: Fran tossing her plaits and ignoring great crowds of lusty, leering, jostling schoolboys as they vie for her attention, burying her pert nose in yet another volume of Shakespeare.

For the first time it occurs to me that Fran might actually get off on all the attention. I correct myself.

She's my best friend, after all.

She wouldn't act all devious like that, Fran.

Would she?

Chapter Thirteen

Things go from bad to worse.

'When are you getting out of here?' Fran's saying.

We've been up in my room for over two hours now, struggling to find things to say to one another. We never used to have this problem at school. At school we got told off for whispering in the back of the biology lab. There was always so much to say. Lessons got in the way of our need for constant communication. If we weren't whispering, we were texting. If we weren't texting, we were emailing.

Now I'm struggling to find anything in

common. Forest Hill House has got between us and thrown everything into a new light.

'It must be like so annoying being stuck here with all these weird people,' says Fran, just as I'm about to make some rubbish comment about the weather.

I flush. If they're weird, then I must be weird too, because we're all living together.

I glance out of the window. Lib and Alice appear as two small dots at the end of the road, on their way back to Forest Hill.

'They might be weird, but they're just people trying to sort out their issues,' I say. 'In the same way as I'm trying to sort out mine.'

'Well, I hope you don't mind me saying, but to be honest your habits were getting a bit much,' says Fran.

I can hardly believe what I'm hearing.

'I mean – all that stuff about not touching the seat on the bus and taking your own cutlery everywhere. Everyone in class was talking about it.'

'I thought . . .' I begin. Tears are rising up, uninvited. I take a deep breath. 'I thought you understood.'

'Not really,' says Fran. 'I tried, but it was difficult hanging around the loos all the time waiting for you to wash your hands three million times.'

Oh, I think. *Now it's all coming out.*

By this point I've got off the bed and am standing by the window.

'Slight exaggeration,' I say. 'I don't wash anything three million times.'

Fran has stood up too. The air between us crackles, black and unfriendly.

Marilyn Manson is roaring something about life being shit next door.

Couldn't have put it better myself, Mazza, I think.

I look at my best friend in her expensive Gap

clothes and with her prudish, hurt expression and I want to scream and rip the dress off her and stamp on it. Except that that would involve bodily contact, of course.

I sink back on to the bed, exhausted. Perhaps she's right. I am a weirdo. My stepmother's thrown me out of the house. I can't touch anything without a tissue being involved. I carry my own knife and fork in my jeans. I jump hundreds of times a day until my feet are swollen and I scrub my face until it's bleeding.

The session with the Doc fades. I touched the Toilet of Doom and then Fran turned up and it was a different Fran, poking fun and being shallow.

The Doc has got it all wrong. I touched dirt and then this happened. I've screwed up – again.

'I think you'd better go,' I say to Fran.

Her eyes widen.

'Me?' she says. 'But it's not me who's got the

problem. I came all this way to see you!'

'Fran,' I say, 'you could have come from Bongo-Bongo land and I'd still be telling you to go.'

She edges towards the door, tears bubbling up in her eyes.

I swallow hard at this. I've hurt her, but not as much as she's hurt me.

'You are so going to regret this,' she says.

'I'm *so* telling you to get the hell out of my room,' I shoot back at her.

I watch the last remnants of my old life crumble and die.

Then I go to the sink and scrub at my face until bits of soap and skin mingle with blood and turn pink on the brush.

Heather comes up ten minutes later.

'Knock knock,' she says, bouncing inside and giving me some 'mwah mwah' air-kisses. She appraises my shredded face with a knowing nod.

'Why are you pretending to knock when you've just barged in anyway?' I say, coughing on clouds of Chanel.

I'm morphing into Caro with my new grumpy behaviour.

'Watch it, kiddo,' says Heather. 'I've left a fashion editor screaming for my head on a plate so that I could get here.'

Today she's wearing tight black leather trousers, the red leather jacket, bright red glass dangly earrings and the spike-heeled black boots.

'Nice place Erin's got here, isn't it?' she says. It takes me a moment to remember who Erin is.

'It's OK,' I say. My head is spinning. Heather takes up a lot of air space with her bright colours and heady perfume. I open the window.

'I hear you've settled in well,' she says. 'And Erin told me about what you achieved earlier. Well done, you!'

I give a weak smile. I love Heather but I'm getting tired of bright shiny perfect people coming into my room. I want to huddle up in the window seat, like Caro does, and think about Mum before she got ill and Dad before Mum died.

I want Lib and Alice to come back from their shopping expedition and tip out their CDs and charity-shop bargains all over my floor (well away from my feet, of course).

I even want to go and see how Caro is doing. The Manson has been turned off and there's silence, but I sense that she's still in there. Listening through the wall. The thought is oddly comforting.

'Does my stepmother really know I'm here?' I ask Heather.

To give her credit, Heather refrains from flushing or fiddling, like Fran did.

'Yes,' she says. 'I could hardly carry on

163

pretending you were in the local hospital or she'd have turned up there to visit you.'

'How did she take it?' I say.

'Surprisingly well,' says Heather. 'But I warn you – she'll want to come here and see you soon.'

I look back into the room from where I've been staring out of the window and it seems different, smaller, not mine. I wonder who will stay in here when I've gone.

'She can't make me go home, can she?' I say. My voice has shrunk to a wobbly whisper.

Heather sighs.

'Your stepmum can do whatever she likes, kiddo,' she says. 'She is your only legal guardian, after all, unless your father manages to . . .'

She starts and puts her hand over her mouth.

'What?' I say. 'Manages to what? Do you know where he is?'

Heather zips up her leather jacket and gives me her bright smile.

'Never mind,' she says. 'I'm just wittering on as usual.'

I miss Dad so much that I feel sick.

Heather and Fran leave soon after and I wave them off from the front doorstep with the Doc standing behind me, but this time I'm glad to see the red Porsche roar away.

Josh comes up the steps with bundles of steaming paper under his arm.

'Fish and chips,' he says. 'Thought we'd give Caro's birthday one last shot.'

I run upstairs and wash my face another thirty-one times. I screw on my longest, most expensive dangly bright blue earrings and put on my favourite cut-off jeans and a tight white T-shirt.

It's one in the eye for Fran. If she saw the length of my earrings she'd know that I was happy to see her walk out of my life once and for all.

I toss my head.

My defiant earrings sparkle and swing against my neck.

The girls come down with their shopping bags as I'm helping Josh divide out the fish and chips on to plates and wishing I could sneak some of the gooey ones stuck on the paper into my mouth but that would be major Germ Alert.

'That market was awesome,' says Lib, dumping carrier bags on to the kitchen table. Alice is smiling in her uncertain way and there's even a small spot of colour on her cheese-slicer cheekbones.

'Presents,' says Lib. She's thought of everyone.

'For you, you bossy old cow,' she says to the Doc, passing her a tea towel with 'I'm the boss' emblazoned in red on the front.

'And you, hippy man,' she says to Josh. His

present is a tiny horn hanging from a black leather cord.

'Right on,' says Josh, tying it round his neck and giving her his sweet, sleepy smile.

'Princess,' says Lib, handing me a package. She's bought me a selection pack of cheap cleaning products that say '99p' and a pink sparkly magic wand.

'Perfect,' I say, brandishing the wand in her direction.

'And these are for Silent Sol,' says Lib, unwrapping a packet of his favourite cigarettes, 'but I see he hasn't graced us with his moody presence.'

'Zelah, run up and give Sol a good hard knock, would you?' says the Doc.

Her words hang in the air. I blush as I catch Lib and Alice exchange raised suggestive eyebrows.

'She'd *love* to,' says Lib.

I pull my elbows in and do my usual stair climb, avoiding the banisters. I stop at the top, do my one hundred and twenty-eight jumps and check my reflection in the mirror.

Whether it's the jumping, or all the mixed emotions of the afternoon, or the fact that I've been given a present, or that the fish and chips smell amazing, my eyes are all watery and sparkly. Even my unruly black hair looks OK, tied back into a pony to show off the long blue earrings.

I stick my chest out a bit, assume my best smile and knock on Sol's door.

No answer.

I try again and there's still no answer, so I say, 'Hello?' and push open the door.

His room smells of boy mixed with man: trainers and the sour whiff of unwashed duvet topped by a stronger odour of shower-gel and just-rolled cigarettes.

On the wall there are posters of Pamela Anderson, Gwen Stefani, Goldfrapp and Sarah Michelle Gellar dressed up as Buffy.

'So he likes them blonde, sleek and glamorous,' I say to my dark and frazzled reflection. 'Oh well.'

Sol is nowhere in sight so I'm just about to go downstairs and satisfy the screaming hunger in my belly by sinking my front teeth into a nice piece of crispy cod, when an envelope catches my eye.

I recognise Sol's thick, angry scrawl and wrap a tissue round my hand so that I can pick it up.

The really weird thing is what it says on the envelope.

The envelope is addressed to me.

Josh is whacking the gong in an effort to get everyone back at the table.

'It's all going cold,' he complains as I run

downstairs breathless after another series of jumps.

'Well, where is he?' says the Doc. 'Don't tell me he's gone out somewhere. He knew we were doing a special supper.'

'He'll probably come back when he gets hungry,' I say, trying to keep my voice steady.

'Maybe. I give up!' says the Doc as Josh splashes a large amount of blackcurrant-coloured wine into her glass.

She flaps her hands as if batting away any further problems and cradles the glass with a heavy sigh.

'He'll come back when he's ready,' says Lib. She's quieter than usual, fiddling with the strings on her sweatshirt, plaiting them and sucking the ends.

'Sol's such an idiot,' says Caro. She's drinking Coke from a can and shovelling chips into her face, lounging back in her chair with a challenging look on her face. It says, *I've only come down because I'm hungry and you're lucky to have me here at all.*

Sol's letter crackles in the side pocket of my jeans. I'm itching to know what it says, but the mound of steaming golden chips on my plate is making me faint with hunger.

Stomach first, letter later.

When Josh has cleared away the last of the greasy plates and everyone is congratulating Alice for eating five chips and a whole mouthful of fish, I slip away upstairs to my room.

I sit in the window and open Sol's letter with a clean tissue wrapped round my fingers. In the light from the streetlamp his writing looks sparse and black against the cream-coloured page.

'Zelah,' it says as a prefix. No 'Dear Zelah' or 'Gorgeous stunning lovely Zelah', just plain 'Zelah'.

I read the note straight through. It's only a few lines long. This is what it says:

Zelah. I'm telling you this because you've lost your mother too and you know what it feels like. I can't stay here any longer because I don't fit in. I can't go home because Dad shouts all the time and I'm scared I'll lose it and hit him. I'll be OK. Please don't tell Josh and the Doc about me going. I need time to get as far away as possible. I might head towards Exeter. Got mates there. Good luck with the OCD thing. You'll beat it. Sol.

This is the first time I've ever heard Sol's voice, even though it's in a letter. The voice is scared and angry all at the same time.

I wonder how the rain has got through the window and then I realise I'm crying. Great big silent tears. All the stuff from today is coming out through my eyes and running down my chin.

I see Fran's face again, in slow motion: the hurt look and how small she seemed when she turned and walked away. All those years of being best friends at school now seem like a complete sham. Fran thinks I'm a weirdo and she's only just found the words to tell me.

I hear Caro's screams of frustration and see Alice's starved unhappy face.

I see Sol's empty room with the blue duvet and the posters.

I see Lib as she looked earlier, stripped of her cheerful mask, naked and vulnerable underneath.

I see Dad's face that last time as he got into the car holding his briefcase as usual, looking as if he was driving to school.

I see myself, waiting at the window for him to come home from work while my stepmother fussed about in the kitchen behind me.

I hear the clock ticking past every hour until it was bedtime and he still hadn't come.

I catch the roar of Heather's car and see her glamorous red-lipped grin and swinging hair.

I see, fainter now, Mum's pretty round face and curly dark hair in the days before the chemo made it all fall out.

She's fading. Every day that goes by, the image fades a little more. I'm terrified that one day I won't be able to summon it up at all.

'Sol,' I whisper. 'You've got to come back. If you come back, I promise I'll listen to you. I understand. About your mum, and all that.'

I almost expect to hear him walk up the front path and through the front door.

The only sound is the drip-drip of rain from the gutter above my window.

I tuck the letter under my pillow and head for the sink.

My rituals go on for hours that night.

Chapter Fourteen

It doesn't take long for the Doc to get worried about Sol going missing.

When I come down for breakfast the next morning, she's sitting at the kitchen table with a policeman and a small, thin bloke who looks like Sol only a lot older. The man has leathery brown skin, a gold chain round his neck and a tiny gold stud in one ear. He's wearing a battered dark-brown suede jacket and a lot of dark stubble.

'Oh, Zelah,' says the Doc in a distracted voice. There are violet circles under her eyes and her hair is wilder than usual. 'This is Sol's father, Gino. Sol didn't come back last night.'

Sol's father extends a hand in my direction. I smile and shake my head.

'Zelah doesn't do handshaking,' explains the Doc.

The man makes a small nodding head gesture. It says, Oh, right, but his eyes say, *Not another screwed up teenager.*

'You know where my boy is?' he says in a weird accent, Cockney with a bit of foreign thrown in. 'Only he don't talk an awful lot so it's kinda hard to know what's going on in dat head of his.'

I busy myself making toast.

'Zelah's only been here for a couple of weeks,' says the Doc. 'She's new.'

At that moment Josh slopes in and the focus of the conversation shifts away from me.

I slip away back upstairs.

*

Sol doesn't turn up that day. Or the next. Or for another whole four days after that. The policeman comes back twice. The Doc and I have another therapy session, but her eyes have a distant, preoccupied look in them. She tells me to cut my jumps down to half if I can, but her ear is listening out for the sound of the telephone or the ring of the doorbell.

Lib, Alice and I are sitting in my room when Caro pops her head round the door. 'I reckon he's jumped off Beachy Head or something,' is her cheerful conclusion. 'Oh well. At least we won't have to put up with all that moody silence any more.'

Lib is looking at Caro as if she is a tiny slug who's just crawled up out of a festering pile of dung.

She's stopped smiling for the last couple of days. Without the grin her face looks harder, less girlish. I can see what she'll look like when she's sixty.

'Sol wasn't quiet because he was moody,' she says. 'If anyone's moody around here, it's you, Caro.'

'Yeah, yeah,' says Caro. 'Whatever. You believe what you want, Lib. You just stay in your nice cosy little world of make-believe.'

Alice scuttles out of the room with her head bent and her hands shoved in her pockets.

'Now look what you've done,' says Lib. 'Was that really necessary?'

Caro gives a short, hard laugh.

'So I've frightened the resident mouse,' she says. 'So what? She'll go and nibble her way through a microgram of cheese or something.'

She bangs out of the room.

Lib sits next to me on the window seat with a shake of her head.

'You're quiet, Princess,' she says. 'Don't take

any notice of Caro. She's pissed off because she's not the centre of attention at the moment.'

I look into Lib's grey eyes and feel the crackle of Sol's letter in my pocket.

'Why can't Sol talk?' I say.

Lib hoists her legs up into the window seat and hugs her knees in their grey combats. I notice for the first time that her hands are trembling, the nails bitten right down, leaving bits of sore red skin visible.

'Yeah, he can,' she says. 'He only talks when he feels completely safe with someone.'

'Has he ever talked to you, or the Doc?' I say. I can't imagine not talking. Words just kind of burst out of my mouth, even when I don't want them to.

'No,' says Lib. 'We've never heard his voice. Ever.'

I think of Sol, hitch-hiking his way down the motorway in total silence. How will he buy a train ticket in Exeter or get a room in a hostel if he can't speak? I picture his small dark form curled up on a park bench somewhere, with nothing to eat or drink and my heart begins to ache. I push the window open and take a deep gulp of air.

'You sure you're all right?' says Lib. 'You're acting a bit weird.'

'Fine,' I say. Then just as she's leaving the room I blurt it out.

'Lib,' I say. My words come out in a great rushing string of babble. 'I know where Sol has gone only he told me not to tell anyone and now even though I should tell someone I've kind of gone past that stage and I know I'm in big trouble but . . .'

Lib is gesturing for me to shut up.

'Zelah,' she says, 'if you know where Sol has gone you have to tell the Doc. Right now. She's out of her head with worry.'

I follow her out of the room with a sinking feeling in my stomach.

'For God's sake you can do that later,' says Lib as I stop to do my jumps on the top step.

With a superhuman effort I stop jumping and go down to the kitchen. I make a mental note that I need to do ninety-eight more jumps later to make up the complete set.

The Doc is watering her indoor plants and gazing out into the back garden, frowning. The policeman is back and sitting at the table with Josh and Sol's dad. There's a photograph of Sol on the table. I catch sight of the dark eyes and olive skin and feel a great whooshing sinking sensation in my stomach.

'Zelah's got something to tell you,' says Lib, launching straight in.

She flaps her hands at me.

Gino's filmy, tired eyes stare up at me. Josh turns his sleepy gaze upon me. The Doc swivels round from the kitchen sink with a red plastic watering can in her hand.

'Go on, tell them,' hisses Lib.

The policeman licks his finger and ruffles through his notepad to find a clean page.

'Sol left me a note,' I say, in a small voice. Then I put my hands up over my face to shield the barrage of questions about to come my way.

Lots of things happen very fast. Sol's father grabs the note from my hand. He brushes my fingers with his own and I feel sick with panic but the Doc is blocking my passage to the sink.

The policeman scans the note over Gino's shoulder and then starts to fire off orders into his walkie-talkie as he heads off towards his car.

Gino shakes hands with the Doc and Josh, grabs his jacket and follows the policeman.

I stand by the kitchen table with tears pouring down my face and plopping on to my silver flip-flops.

The Doc gestures for me to sit down.

'You should have told us straight away,' she says. Her face is cold and stern behind the glasses. 'I thought you had more sense than that, Zelah.'

'I do,' I say, snorting up snot and feeling around my jeans for a tissue before it drips on my clothes and contaminates them.

'Here you are, honey,' says Josh, chucking me a packet. The gesture makes me cry even more.

'Don't be too hard on her,' he says to the Doc. 'Sol did make her promise not to tell. You know what the kids are like with loyalty.'

The Doc nods in silence and fiddles with her charm bracelet. When she looks at me again, her eyes are kinder.

'Well, at least you told us in the end,' she says. 'I'm sure the police will find Sol now.'

I find Lib waiting for me outside my bedroom.

'You did the right thing,' she says. She's already making off downstairs towards her own room. Lib is spending more and more time closeted away from the rest of us. I haven't heard the Arctic Monkeys blaring out for ages.

I think of Sol's dark haunted eyes and sad note. I shiver. He's going to kill me if the police bring him back here.

'I hope so, Lib,' I say to her retreating back. 'I really hope so.'

That evening something weird happens.

I never finish off my jumps.

I pass the top stair and hesitate for a moment.

Then I just keep on walking, up to my bedroom.

I feel a bit sick and floaty and as if some large heavy thing is missing from my evening, but I just scrub my face and hands instead.

I'm still doing this at half-ten when I hear the

heavy click of the front door downstairs.

The Doc is talking to somebody in the hall. Her voice rises in anger and then dips down into a consoling murmur. There's another click and out of the window I see the policeman take off his hat and walk back down the front path in a slow, relaxed sort of way.

I know in a flash.

Sol's been found.

I hear Alice run downstairs and Lib's slower footsteps following. Caro stays in her room. She turns up the music a fraction louder.

I stay rooted on my bed, eyes upon the door. Any minute now it's going to open and Sol's going to burst in and attack me with his eyes flashing and his arms flailing about.

I wait.

The clock ticks past eleven.

I wait a bit more.

I decide to lie down on the duvet. Might as well be comfortable before I meet my death.

The next thing I know I'm pulled out of sleep by a nameless invisible presence.

I reach for my lamp.

Sol is glaring at me from the foot of my bed.

Chapter Fifteen

He looks dreadful.

His bomber jacket is splattered with mud and there's a large hole in the knee of his jeans. His face is haggard and there's dark stubble on his top lip and chin.

'Oh, you're back, then,' I say, like an idiot. I struggle into a sitting position and clutch my pink pyjamas across my chest in case they're gaping open. In the mirror I can see that my hair is all flat on one side and sticking up in a horrid peak on the other.

Sol doesn't speak. He just carries on looking at me. I can't read the look. It's not anger,

187

but he's not smiling either.

'I'm really sorry,' I say. 'I had to tell them. They were getting in a real state about you. Your father was . . .'

At the mention of his father Sol gets up and walks over to my attic window. He places his hands on the sill and grips it, shoulders tense and hunched, back turned towards me.

Then he turns around and feels in his pocket, producing a scrap of paper and a pen. He scrawls something and hands it to me. I can't take it, so he drops it on the bed instead.

I thought I could trust you, it says. *I thought you understood. You lost your mother too!*

He's heading for the door. I can't leave it like that.

'Hey, I do understand,' I say. My voice is all crusty and low, full of sleep.

Sol snatches the paper back and adds something on the other side.

You don't know what it's like living with my father,
it says.

I think of Gino with his dark eyes like Sol's
and his gold earring.

'He was really worried about you,' I say. 'He
was here every day asking questions.'

Sol laughs at this, a soundless laugh that
involves his shoulders jerking up and down and
his mouth opening and closing.

He grabs my diary off the bedside table and
rips out a blank sheet.

'Hey,' I protest, but only in a quiet voice. The
way Sol's looking, I know I'm in no position to
wind him up.

Sol passes me the paper. I wrap a tissue
round my hand, take it between my thumb and
fingernail and hold it under the lamp.

I'll tell you how much my father cares about me, it
says. *Enough to kill my mother right in front of me.*
That's how much.

189

Then he sinks down on to the floor and puts his hands over his head and starts to shake.

It's past midnight and I'm sitting on the wooden floorboards of my room without even a towel beneath my cold buttocks in their thin pyjamas and I'm sitting as close to Sol as possible without actually touching him.

I want to touch him, though. In my head I see another Zelah. Not the podgy-cheeked squashy-haired one with the flat chest. This is another taller, more beautiful Zelah with a bigger chest and lovely smooth dark hair. In my head this Zelah has got her arms round Sol and he's got his head on her shoulder and she can feel all the warmth of his hard, thin body pressed up against her . . .

Like that's ever going to happen.

There are about a million bits of paper

scattered around our feet. On them lies the story of Sol's life.

He's told me how his parents used to run an Italian restaurant in London and how they were happy even though they had screaming rows and chucked big white plates at one another.

He's told me about his dad saving up two years to buy a sports car because he was car mad and how his dad used to wash and polish that car every Sunday afternoon until you could see your reflection in the bonnet.

He's told me how, after one of their screaming rows, his father stormed out to the car and slammed the gears into reverse so that he could go for a drive around the block to cool down.

He's told me about the scream and the heavy thump against the back of the car and the horrible moment of complete silence before his father got out, yelling his mother's name, and ran into the road.

He's told me how he watched all this, aged ten, from the front doorstep.

He saw the limpness of his mother's head as she dangled from his father's arms. Heard the roaring and crying coming from his father. Witnessed the panic to dial 999 and the wait for the ambulance.

Sol saw the body being carried away under a green sheet.

They covered up her face, he wrote. I never saw her again. That was the day I lost my voice.

Light creeps into my bedroom. We've stayed up all night.

I'm telling Sol some of my memories of Dad.

'We used to have a special Father and Daughter Day,' I say. 'The best one was when I was about eight. We went to the Natural History Museum together and saw the stuffed polar bear. Then we sat in the café perched on these really high stools and Dad let me have a bottle of pink Cresta with a straw.'

I pause here for a second. I'm thinking that there must actually have been a time when I'd have just drunk through a straw without thinking about Germ Alert or Dirt Alert first.

Sol grabs another blank page from my diary and writes *When did you stop having the special days?*

That's easy.

'After Mum died,' I say. 'Even though I kind of needed them even more then.'

I tell Sol about Mum and how she lost her hair and grew puffy and yellow and then withered away into a skeleton while Dad drank even more. I tell him about how I've fallen out with Fran and how she's not who I thought she was. The words just keep on pouring out of me. Of course it helps that Sol can't butt in unless he writes something on a scrap of paper. He's a good listener.

As weak strains of sunlight begin to filter in over my floorboards I hear the Doc go downstairs and fill the kettle.

Sol makes to stand up, unsteady. I catch a whiff of sweat and tobacco and stale clothing.

Then I do something really weird. Something I haven't done for years.

I reach out and grab his hand for a moment. The skin feels cold, smooth and stretchy under my fingers.

'You'll be OK,' I say, letting go of the hand.

I wade through bits of crumpled paper and hop back beneath my cold duvet. It's six in the morning and I have to get up in two hours to begin my rituals.

Sol nods and walks towards the door, yawning.

He stops just before opening it. He turns to where I'm already half asleep in my bed and gives me a grin.

'Hey, Zelah,' he says in a deep gruff voice.

I jump out of my skin.

'Thanks.'

Chapter Sixteen

After that night with Sol, things are OK between us.

He still refuses to speak in front of the others, but if we meet on the stairs he barks out a brief, 'Hi,' and gives me a scowling smile.

He's lent me his iPod without me asking and after I've done therapy he makes a point of sticking his head round my bedroom door and asking me if I'm OK.

It's not just Sol who's getting better. Everyone is thrilled with Alice because the Sunday after Sol gets back she eats a small bowl of cereal and manages to keep it down. Her reward is another small bowl of muesli for supper but she eats that too, flushing with effort, encouraged by Josh.

Lib's still up in her room most of the time. I miss her grin and ask the Doc is there's anything wrong, but she just says, 'Lib's working through some issues,' which in this place is about as useful as somebody saying, 'There's weather outside.'

Caro is as grumpy as ever, but she offers to cut my hair at the weekend. My frizzy fringe is so long that I've taken to pinning it up with flowery clips. The result is far from flattering. It exposes my big forehead and makes my face look pale against the black hair.

'She's very good,' says the Doc, seeing my doubtful expression. 'Honestly. She'll take years off you. Not that you really need that, at fourteen.'

'Sit still, will you?' says Caro.

I'm up in her bedroom, sitting on a chair in the middle of the room. Caro's tucked a clean green towel round my shoulders and is snipping away at the split ends and dry sections of my hair.

I've made her dip the scissors in disinfectant and have checked the blades about a hundred times for any specks of dirt.

'OCD, you freak me out, man,' says Caro as she sprays some sort of cold liquid on my head and combs it through. It smells of peaches and blackcurrants.

I watch as little black curls of my hair bounce off my shoulders and drop on to the floor where they lie like shrivelled slugs.

'Don't get in a state — I'll sweep it up,' says Caro, interpreting my expression. She bends down behind me and bites her lip as she concentrates on trimming my hair into a straight line across the tops of my shoulders.

'OK, now we layer it,' she says, coming round to the front and using the very ends of her scissors to cut my hair into shaped sections around my face. They cling to my face in little black feathery strands. As her sleeves fall backwards I can see that Caro's arms are starting to scab over.

'Where'd you learn to cut hair?' I try to imagine Caro working in a salon. Impossible. She'd spit in the coffee and spread vicious gossip between clients before slagging off all the orange-skinned celebrities in the glossy salon magazines.

Then again, perhaps she'd be perfect for the job.

'My mother was a hairdresser,' says Caro. She says this in a very short, unemotional way as if she's saying, 'That'll be three pounds fifty, please,' in a greengrocer's shop. It doesn't invite any further conversation so I sit on my hands and try not to let my flip-flops touch the pile of dead hair on the ground.

When Caro's finished, she looks around for a bottle of styling spray.

'I'll have to borrow one from Lib,' she says. 'Back in a sec.'

I flap my feet up and down and look around, bored.

Caro's room is like that of most teenage girls. CDs lying around in piles, dressing table covered in brushes, bottles and make-up, clothes draped over the bed and packets of tobacco with their lids open, spilling out what looks like dried brown worms.

She's taking ages to come back with the spray.

I get up and wander about. I don't know what makes me crouch down and look under the bed, but I do. I lift the duvet up and peer underneath.

There's a brown box.

I listen for a moment to see if I can hear Caro trudging back upstairs and then I slide the box out and lift the lid.

Inside is Caro's sketchpad.

It's large, with a blue cover. With one ear on the door I wrap a tissue around my hand and flip open the pad to a random page.

My eyes nearly pop out of my head.

The picture is drawn entirely in red. There's a girl with long hair in a dress crouching down at the foot of a bed, tears streaming out of her eyes and her hands clasped together as if in prayer. On top of the bed stands a man beating his chest like an ape. Caro's drawn him in the style of a cartoon so his top half is inflated to giant size and his tiny legs can hardly support him.

Underneath in angry, spiky letters, Caro has given her picture a title.

Our Father, Not in Heaven.

I'm still reeling with shock when I hear Caro coming back upstairs. I shove the pad back in the box and push the whole thing under the bed, fling myself into the chair and pretend to be studying my nails.

Caro's got a white bottle of sticky gunk. She squirts it into her palms and works it through my head, ignoring my squeals of protest.

'It's CLEAN,' she says. 'Honestly, OCD. You drive me demented.'

She picks up a hand mirror and holds it right in front of my face.

I shriek with delight and shock.

Zelah Green the pudding-faced teenager with frizzy black hair has left the building.

A new Zelah blinks back at me. This one has an oval-shaped face with a friendly smile. Her hair is sleek and glossy and just brushes the tops of her shoulders before falling into gentle layers around her face.

I shake my head from side to side, unable to take my eyes off the gorgeous vision in the mirror.

Caro is trying to look disinterested, but a smirk of satisfaction hovers on her lips for a moment.

'See?' she says. 'I'm not all bad.'

I think of the drawing I've just seen and realise that, if Caro is bad, she's been made that way by something terrible.

I want to reach out and touch her damaged arm. Instead, I take off my heart-shaped dangly earrings and hand them to her. I've seen her looking at them when she thinks I'm not concentrating. Mum gave them to me just before she got really ill and they're the most precious things I've got.

I think Mum would have wanted me to do something good with those earrings.

'Payment,' I say.

Caro looks down at the tiny silver hearts nestling in her open palm. She closes her fingers over them and sucks her lips in so that they disappear.

She seems about to speak and then her eyes brim over and she makes a big play of sweeping up locks of hair and folding towels.

I leave her to it.

When the Doc comes up to find me for my session, I'm sitting on my bed thinking about Caro.

'OK, what's up?' she says. 'You look done in. Nice hair, by the way. I like the wavy bits around your face. Very Dorothy Lamour.'

I have no idea who Dorothy Lamour is. I wonder if she was the girl who had this room before me.

'I've seen some of Caro's drawings,' I confess.

The Doc looks concerned. 'So now you know why she's got a lot of anger inside her,' she says. 'But I wish you hadn't looked at the drawings. It might set back your own progress.'

I assure her that it won't. I'm haunted by what I've just seen, but I'm starting to really want to lose my rituals. I've already cut my jumps down to half and stopped checking all the electrical appliances in my bedroom.

I still can't touch anything without a tissue, though. And I'm still doing all the scrubbing and washing.

The Doc wants to work on this today.

She asks me to perform my rituals so that she can observe them.

I feel all self-conscious being watched. I grab the soap and do my right hand, counting to thirty-one, and then my left hand. I finish with a face scrub.

'How did you pick the number thirty-one?'

asks the Doc, leaning back in her chair and gazing at me over the top of her glasses.

'Easy,' I say. 'Mum was thirty-one when she died.'

'Ah,' says the Doc. 'Right. Well – let's pick another important number. Your age next birthday will do.'

She makes me wash my hands fifteen times left, fifteen times right. It only takes a couple of minutes.

'Stress levels out of ten?' she says.

I blot my hands dry on the towel and survey them. They look clean enough.

'Maybe a five?' I say.

She looks pleased and jots something in her book.

'Homework this week, ' she says. 'Wash your hands only fifteen times each, once a day'

'Yes, Miss,' I say. She makes as if to play-cuff my head, remembers just in time and wafts her hand vaguely in front of my face instead.

As she leaves the room, Josh comes in with a brown paper parcel.

'This came for you,' he says, leaving it on my bed.

I wrap a tissue round my hand and rip open the package. Inside is a black box of chocolates with a little red heart-shaped card dangling off it.

My own heart leaps for a second. *Dad?*

The chocolates glisten. Each dark globe is topped with a tiny violet crystal. I select one, pop it in my mouth.

Then I open the card.

See you soon, darling, it says in a familiar scrawl.

I might have known. Dad only ever bought Selection Boxes at Christmas time, not fancy chocolates with ribbons and bows.

Just when things were starting to get better for me.

I run to the sink and spit out a mush of

brown cream into the sink. Then I brush my teeth thirty-one times.

Odd little images of my past life start to run in front of my eyes as I brush my teeth like a lunatic to get rid of the vile tainted chocolate taste.

I remember my stepmother's face as she packed me off in Heather's car.

How she didn't smile or wave as we drove away.

How the month of living alone with her in the house without Dad was like a strange nightmare, both of us going through the motions every day, but secretly wondering what on earth we had in common.

I suppose Dad was the only thing we had in common.

I gargle a big mouthful of nasty-tasting mouthwash.

Then I spit it out as hard as I can.

*

Lib fails to come down at the sound of the lunch gong so Josh goes upstairs to get her.

'She'll go mad if she misses lemon meringue,' says the Doc.

There's the sound of a shout upstairs and then Josh runs downstairs and grabs his coat and car keys with his hair and beard flying all over the place. I've never seen him move so fast.

'Nothing to worry about, just stay in the kitchen,' he throws at me, over his shoulder.

'Zelah, you're in charge,' says the Doc, who's gone white in the face and is following Josh into the hall and grabbing her own coat and bag.

Josh is helping Lib downstairs. I can't see her face but she's mumbling something incoherent and she can't seem to walk very straight.

I watch out of the window as they push Lib into Josh's old estate car and drive off with a screech of tyres.

I sit in silence at the kitchen table with the others.

'Christ,' says Caro, rolling up a cigarette.

I wait for her usual barbed comment.

Nothing more comes out of her mouth.

The Doc and Josh bring Lib home after supper. I've had to cobble together something to eat as I'm in charge so we've all had lumpy beans on charred toast. Nobody complains.

Lib is taken straight up to her room and I ask if I can take her up some of the leftover pudding from lunch.

Josh and the Doc exchange looks.

'Yes, OK,' says Josh. 'But just a quick hello. She's a bit subdued at the moment.'

Lib? Subdued?

I think they must be exaggerating, but when I push open the door of Lib's room and see her lying on her side on the bed with her arms

210

wrapped tight round her stomach as if it hurts, my heart sinks.

'Oh, hi, Princess,' she says. She continues to lie on her side.

'What's up with you?' I say. 'Run out of happy pills?'

Lib's faint smile fades. 'How do you know about that?' she says.

'What?' I say, confused.

She pulls her knees in towards her body until she's huddled up like a foetus.

'Never mind,' she says. 'You'd better get back to your supper, hadn't you?'

It's not a question. It's an order.

I put a plateful of lemon meringue pie on the floor and creep out.

My world is turning black again.

I pop in to see Alice before I go to bed. Josh has decided that she's doing well enough to spend a weekend at home and her parents are about to turn up and take her away in their car.

I sit on the bed and watch her fold up a striped top and place it in a rucksack. She's all dressed up for the occasion in a long black skirt with three layers and a white gipsy blouse.

'Lucky you,' I say. I'm jealous. I've been here for nearly four weeks and it feels like a lot longer. Part of me wishes that Heather would turn up in her red car and whisk me away. But where would I live? Heather's away too often to look after me. My stepmother only wants me around because my problems make her feel better about herself.

And Dad – well, who knows where he might be?

'They're here!' says Alice, watching a green car pull up outside. She gives me her shy look from beneath soft wings of hair. A pleasant-looking couple dressed in Barbour jackets and

Wellingtons get out of a Range Rover and wave up to where Alice is hanging out of the window.

My heart lurches with envy. I know I'm never going to get Mum back again, but I can't help wishing that that was my dad down there, waving up with a proud look in his eyes.

Not that Dad would ever have been able to afford a Range Rover. He drove the same blue Hillman Avenger for about a million years until the bonnet caught fire.

'Have fun,' I say. 'And keep up the muesli. Not literally, of course.'

Alice laughs. I watch her skinny arms hoist the rucksack on to her back.

Maybe Heather will pay me another visit soon.

Heather doesn't come, but the next morning Josh taps on my bedroom door and announces that I'm needed in the kitchen.

It's Sunday so I presume that he wants help with the fry-up. The sun is out and I've managed to stick to my new routine of washing only fifteen times on each side. I insert a pair of green glass dangly earrings into my lobes and brush my new swishy sleek hair into place. I take a pale green T-shirt from the wardrobe and rearrange all the other items so that there are equal spaces in between them.

Then I slide into my favourite skinny jeans and my silver flip-flops and run downstairs, not stopping to jump at the top.

There's a rich smell of ground coffee coming from the kitchen.

'OK, shall I do the eggs and you the bacon?' I say as I burst through the kitchen door.

There's only one person sitting at the table.

Clouds of hair hovering around her head. Thin face, sharp nose.

Her face is tilted towards the door in expectation.

She stands up and holds out her arms.

'Zelah, darling,' she says. 'How are you?'

My stepmother has found her way to Forest Hill House.

Chapter Seventeen

I stop dead and start backing away, but it's too late.

She's up in a flash and is standing with her back against the kitchen door.

No escape.

'Zelah, darling,' she says again, extending her arms towards me. 'Sit down. We need to talk.'

'You know I can't touch you,' I say. I edge towards the sink and lean against it, trying to see whether anyone's in the garden just in case I need to scream.

'You're looking better than I expected,' she says, moving in on me with a critical frown. 'Yes. A lot better.'

Her smile fades a little. She fingers her own flyaway hair.

I'm getting scared. There's nobody around. Where are they all?

'What do you want?' I say. Without moving from the sink I feel around behind me until my fingers brush a wooden spoon. I grasp it hard, shuddering at the feeling of the dry wood on my skin, but even the thoughts of germs invading my body is preferable to another five minutes with my stepmother.

My stepmother has a faint smile hovering on her lips.

'Zelah,' she says. 'Don't be silly. It's not about what I want. It's about what's best for you, of course.'

I'm not buying that one.

'You loathe me,' I hiss. 'Ever since Dad went you've only pretended to like me.'

At the mention of Dad's name her smile fades. She sits down at the kitchen table with a heavy sigh and fumbles in her shiny black bag, rattling a bottle of pills and tipping two into her mouth.

'Life's been very difficult for me,' she says. 'First your father left me and then I was left alone to cope with you and your little, ahem, *problem*.'

'Well, my "little problem" is getting treated now and I'm fine, so could you just go away, please?' I say. I wish that the Doc would bustle into the kitchen in her comforting outsized linen shirt and with her bracelets jangling, or that Josh would amble in and fill the kettle, blinking at me through his half-closed eyes.

My stepmother has stood up again. She's sizing up my hair and clothes with a keen eye.

'Oh, Zelah,' she says. 'It's not that simple, darling. You see – you being in here is very,

very expensive. I could never have afforded these fees.'

Fees?

I'm silent. It's never occurred to me that my place at Forest Hill House costs Actual Money. I kind of assumed that the Doc and Josh were treating kids out of the goodness of their own hearts, but as soon as this thought comes into my head I realise I've been stupid. Of course they have to get paid.

The thought fills me with doubts. Do they really care about me? Am I just another set of bills to be paid? Will they slam the front door shut behind me when I leave and brush off their hands, saying, 'Well, thank goodness she's gone, but at least we've got money for the electric now'? Are we all just customers, like girls visiting a shoe shop except that instead of coming home with a pink box filled with tissue and leather we come home with our brains fixed?

Another more urgent thought breaks through.

'So – who *has* been paying for my treatment, then, if you can't afford the fees? . . . *Dad?*'

'Not likely,' she says. My heart lurches and flips. 'He's too wrapped up in himself to pay your fees.'

So she knows where he is too.

But before I focus on that too much I need to get to the bottom of this thing about the money.

'Who paid the fees, then?' I say.

'Heather,' says my stepmother, spitting the name out like a rancid cherry stone. 'For some reason known only to herself, the woman's fond of you. She told your father she'd pay your fees for the first month.'

I sit down at the table to allow all this information to compute in my head. My thoughts spin all over the place. So . . . Dad knows I'm in here. He hasn't rung up or sent a note or come to visit me. He's had a whole month to find me. He's been speaking to Heather AND my stepmother.

But where is he? What's going on?

'I want to see my father,' I say. 'Right away.'

My stepmother wraps her fur coat round her thin body and stands up.

'Sorry, I can't get hold of him and, anyway, I doubt he'll want to see you,' she says. 'You remind him too much of his old life. Your Mum dying and Heather messing everything up. When I think I'd still be living with him if she hadn't got in the way!'

I can hardly believe what I'm hearing.

Great flames of red anger start to burn before my eyes. I'm starring in one of Caro's cartoons.

'Heather helped Mum, and she's helped me,' I say. 'How can you say that?'

She's shaking her head now.

'It's all in the past now, darling,' she says. 'Anyway, get your bags packed. While your dad's away I'm still responsible for you. You're coming with me.'

My legs begin to tremble. Where *is* everybody? Why isn't Lib coming to my rescue, or the Doc?

'I'm not going home with you,' I manage. 'I've made friends here and they'll look after me. I'm staying.'

My stepmother advances towards me and grips my arm with her black-gloved hand.

I let out a shriek of rage. Nobody, *nobody*, has been allowed to grab my arm for over two years. And now she's got the nerve to just dive in and do it.

I shake my arm free and begin to shout for the Doc, but there's loud music blasting out from upstairs. My stepmother holds up a warning hand in my direction.

'Now look,' she says. 'Stop panicking. I'm not taking you home — I've told you I can't cope with having you in the house. I'm taking you back to the hospital where you should have been in the first place.'

She's invading my personal space and the smell of warm dead animal from her leather glove too near my mouth is starting to make me feel like becoming an emergency vegetarian.

'Get away from me!' I scream. 'I'm not going to the hospital! It'll finish me off!'

Of course. That's what she wants. To finish me off properly so that my rituals get worse and she can commit me forever to a psychiatric unit and then she can wash her hands of me completely.

'Hey look,' I say. 'I must be getting better. Because I can do – this!'

I push her aside with all my might and manage to fling open the kitchen door.I slap down the tiled hallway in my flip-flops and heave open the front door, intending to run towards the motorway and flag down a passing truck or something, but I don't reckon on Josh coming up the front drive holding a chest of drawers.

I see him, but it's too late – I'm already smashing into the wood and there's a dull pain across the front of my

head.

'I hope that wood's clean,' I say, clutching my head and looking behind in a panic. *Where's my stepmother gone?*

Josh is kind of looming towards me with a look of concern in his eyes.

'Here, let me see your head, honey,' he's saying.

Then it all goes black.

Chapter Eighteen

My first thought when I open my eyes and see the hall light dangling over my face is this:

Oh, great. I spend all that effort trying to run away and now I'm still here.

My first word is less clear.

'Whaaappenned?'

I'm trying to look around me but my eyes are covered in some sort of blurry cling-film and the only thing I can see is a big white moon-faced thing looming up towards me with empty black eye-sockets.

I flap my hands at it in fear.

'G'way, thing,' I mumble.

The white moon face hovers for a moment and then slinks back to whatever dank dark coffin-studded vault it's come from.

'Jesus, OCD,' says a cross voice. 'Chill. Just trying to be loving and caring. OK – I admit it's a long shot.'

Caro.

I try and focus in the direction of the voice.

'Why do you look like a vampire?' I whisper.

There's a short, rough snort of amusement.

'You're looking at my T-shirt,' she says. 'At least – I hope you are.'

The sinister features of Marilyn Manson swim back into view.

'Oh, thank God,' I say. 'I thought I was in the Underworld.'

'Welcome to my life,' says Caro. She's grinning at me now, a most unexpected phenomenon. Her teeth are tiny, white and vulnerable-looking.

I didn't even know she had any.

'You look pretty when you smile,' I say. I must be concussed or something but I can't stop. 'Kind of – more girly and less grumpy.'

Caro stops grinning and reverts back to her old scowl.

I realise I'm lying on the cold black-and-white tiled floor of the hallway and try to sit up in a panic. *Major Dirt Alert!* All that mud off people's boots sticking to my back and my bottom and my head can't be good for me.

'Whoa, take it easy,' says Josh. 'Don't move, just in case. Erin's ringing NHS Direct for advice.'

'Huh?' I mumble. 'Whassafor?'

'You ran into my new piece of Art Deco,' says Josh. 'Shame really. It's dented now, beyond repair. Only kidding.'

I'm struggling to remember what happened.

'Why was I running?' I say.

'Well, I met some uptight woman in the hall who said she was your stepmother,' says Caro.

A great chill washes up from my feet to my head. All the blurriness vanishes and my head feels as clear as day.

'Where – where is she?' I whisper.

Caro goes into the kitchen and comes back with a glass of squash. I hold my hand out but she drinks it herself.

'Disappeared,' she says.

'Eh?' I say. Nothing is making sense.

I can feel tears pricking up at the edges of my eyes. My head aches and my eyes still feel a bit blurry.

'My stepmother,' I say, remembering. 'She tried to get me to leave here and go to a mental hospital.'

Josh frowns.

'That lovely woman?' he says. 'I let her in. I thought she was charming.'

I tell him what happened in the kitchen.

Josh crouches down next to my head, shaking his head in disbelief.

'Oh, Zelah,' he says. 'Why didn't you call for help? I feel I've let you down. We've all been so busy keeping an eye on Lib that we haven't given you much attention.'

''S OK,' I manage.

The main thing is that my stepmother seems to have disappeared off the face of the planet.

The NHS Direct lady says I should stay in bed and be checked for mild concussion.

The Doc sends me straight to my room.

'No hopping out to do rituals,' she says. 'If you really have to, call me in and you can sit up in bed with a basin.'

She switches on my bedside lamp and closes the door behind her.

I lie for three hours, all dried-up and hopeless,

in my white bed with a tray of Marmite sandwiches next to me and I try to think.

Where will I go when I'm better?

I can't stay here any longer because of the money.

I can't go home, and my stepmother seems to have disappeared anyway.

As I'm running through the list of bleak possibilities – *Orphanage? Workhouse? Factory? Cardboard box?* – the door to my bedroom creaks open and a familiar red head of streaky blonde highlights pops round it.

'Sorry it took me so long to get here, kiddo,' it says. 'The traffic on that A road! I've got through a five-CD Madonna box set!'

I laugh, for the first time that evening. It hurts my head, but it feels good.

Heather perches on the edge of my bed and dispenses glossy magazines, Lucozade, expensive toiletries and classy bars of organic chocolate.

'Should keep you going for a bit,' she says. She casts a look of disgust at the Marmite sandwiches.

Her small act of kindness has set me off blubbing again, and when Heather sees my tragic soon-to-be-an-orphan expression, she starts off as well so that in the end we're both snorting and sniffling and laughing and going puce in the face.

'Oh boy, do we need chocolate,' she says, snapping off half a bar and shoving it into her mouth. Then she shoves the other half into mine.

We stuff in chocolate until we feel ill. Then Heather plumps up my pillows and washes my face and hands with a cold wet flannel.

'Thanks,' I say. It feels brilliant, having my hands washed. There's no chance of me doing any rituals while I'm under strict instructions from the Doc.

'Need to look your best, might have a visitor,' she says. She's kind of fidgety and anxious and keeps looking at the door.

My heart leaps. Is Sol about to come in and act out a major romance at my bedside? Him all dark and swarthy and passionate, me all frail and pale and lost-looking against my white cotton sheets?

'Earrings!' I say. Heather understands. She unhooks the big gold hoops from her ears and washes them in the sink. Then she slots them into my ears. Even though they're not my style, I feel better straight away.

'OK, let him in,' I say, adopting what I hope is a come-hither, winning smile.

Heather gives me a puzzled look.

'How did you know?' she says.

'Know what?' I say, but by then she's already by the door, beckoning someone to come in.

A dark figure blocks out the light for a moment.

Sol must have grown about two feet taller and bulked up. Perhaps he's been working out at the gym. Or maybe he has become a seventies dancer and has platform shoes on. A whole host of delirious post-concussion thoughts follow onto these ones.

The figure advances towards the bed and only then do I get a whiff of a familiar smell: Old Spice aftershave mingled with musty wood chippings, leather and just a hint of that peculiar sort of dry shampoo that smells like talcum powder.

I try to hold out my arms, but they're pinned beneath the sheets because Heather is sitting on them so instead I just yell as loud as I can.

The Doc and Josh come running in, primed for emergency medical action, but I don't care.

I scream and scream until my lungs ache.

'Dad!'

Chapter Nineteen

Dad leans over to plant a very slow, soft, deliberate kiss on my forehead.

I shake my head in panic. He remembers and stands up straight with a nervous cough. He's wearing a red-checked shirt and jeans with Timberland boots, just like he always used to, but the skin underneath his eyes is all white and papery.

'Dad,' I say again. I can't seem to say anything else.

My dad. Here in this very room.

'Hello, Princess,' he says. My eyes flood again and when I've finished crying I explain about

Lib and how she called me that too and how she's been so sick.

Dad listens, patting the side of my bed and nodding.

'I'm here now,' he keeps saying, over and over.

Heather has faded into the background, but she's grinning like mad and sticking her thumbs up in my direction in between scoffing the last chocolates.

'How did you find Dad?' I ask her.

My father and Heather exchange a glance.

'Zelah, I've known where your father was all along,' Heather says. 'He sent me the money for your treatment.'

I look from her to him and back again. This isn't making sense.

'But where've you been, Dad? Didn't you want to know what was happening to me? And how come you didn't visit me?'

'Because,' says Dad, taking a deep shaky

breath, 'because I was getting some treatment of my own.'

Heather has come over to the bed and put her arm round his shoulders.

'What treatment?' I say.

Dad has buried his face in his hands.

Heathers turns to face me.

'Your dad got a bit too fond of the bottle,' she says. 'Because of your mum dying and your illness.'

Of course.

I remember the smell of stale beer on his breath and then a little film rewinds in my head: Dad unloading lots of wine bottles from the shopping bags and stuffing them into the sideboard and under the sink when he thought I wasn't looking. Dad coming home late from the pub, my stepmother's disapproving glare and the smell of cigarettes and whisky clashing with the smell of peach air freshener in the bathroom.

'So where have you been for the past month?' I say. My voice is cold and unfriendly, but I can't help it.

Dad clears his throat.

'I've been getting some help in a treatment centre,' he says. 'Trying to beat this so that I could be stronger for you.'

'Oh,' I say. 'But – why didn't you text me, then?'

'No phones allowed in the place,' says Dad. 'We were only allowed to write letters.'

'So why didn't you write me any?' I say. 'All the time I was still living at home, you could have written me letters.'

Dad comes out from behind his hands.

'I did,' he says. 'Loads of them. Your step-mother hid them in a drawer. God knows why. I only found them this evening when I was discharged from the hospital and went home.'

I gesture towards the bottle of Lucozade.

My lips are drier than toast.

Heather pours me out a glassful and passes it to me with a clean tissue wrapped round the rim.

I sink my face into the mass of soft orangey bubbles.

'So why did you marry her, then?' I say. 'What was the point of that?'

Dad sighs and looks out of my window at the streetlights.

'I was a bit of a mess after your mother died,' he says. 'I suppose I just got swayed by a pretty face. Your stepmother can be very charming.'

'Huh,' I say. I've not seen much evidence of it, myself.

'So why did you leave her?' I persist. I need to make sense of all this.

My dad exchanges another look with Heather.

'I didn't leave,' he says. 'Your stepmother got fed up of my drinking and booted me out.

If it hadn't been for Heather's help, I'd have gone to pieces.'

A big clonk sounds in my head as a giant piece of puzzle falls into place.

'Hang on,' I say. 'You and Heather. You're an item, aren't you?'

I don't want to ask him how long he's loved her for, but Dad reads my mind in that spooky parent way.

'It started after your mum died, not before,' he says. 'And I think and hope that your mum would have approved,' he continues. 'She was very fond of Heather.'

That's true enough. I'm fond of her too. I'm fast running out of reasons to be cross with him now so I give them both a cautious smile.

'She's a bit young for you, though, Dad,' I say.

'And I am NOT going to be your surrogate mother, kiddo,' says Heather.

We laugh together in a nervous kind of way.

Chapter Twenty

I leave Forest Hill House two weeks later. The Doc's referred me to a local unit nearer home where I can attend as a day patient.

She comes to see me off, along with Josh, Sol, Caro and Lib. Alice has been allowed to return home to her parents for good so she's not around, but she rang me up on my mobile and in her shy, quiet voice wished me lots of luck.

Sol steps forward and gives me a hug, which doesn't actually involve touching. Although I rather wish it did.

'I'll write you a letter,' he says.

Then he reaches out and holds my hand for a second. And I let him.

The Doc and Josh stare in disbelief both at the unfamiliar sound of Sol's voice and the sight of me gripping flesh with no tissue for protection.

I see them give each other a quick smile.

I go all pink and tears well up in my eyes.

Caro makes vomiting noises and grins. She's got softer over the last week, like all her sharp edges have turned into curved ones. She gives me one of her less shocking cartoons as a parting gift. It shows a red-cheeked girl with frizzy black hair and long dangly earrings holding out a long sword towards a giant toilet. The bowl has eyes and fangs. The picture is entitled *Zelah Battles the Toilet of Doom*.

'Good luck, OCD,' she says.

Lib is hanging back, awkward, staring down at her trainers.

'Virtual hug, Princess?' She puts her arms round me in a big circle without touching me.

Tears spring up in my eyes at the comforting whiff of green parka, cigarette smoke and hair gel.

'Don't do anything stupid,' I manage to croak.

Lib grins. It's not quite her old grin but it's the best I've seen in ages. Maybe she will get better.

The Doc knows better than to try and hug me, but she gazes down at me with her kind, bright eyes.

'You'll get there, Zelah,' she says.

Josh gives me a little bow, yawning, and a sleepy wink.

'Take care of yourself, honey,' he says.

The five of them stand outside the tall white house on the top step as I get into the back of Heather's red Porsche. Dad and Heather are sitting in the front. There's not really any back seat so I'm sitting in the boot, but I don't mind.

I watch the Doc, Josh, Lib, Caro and Sol out of the back window until they are just five tiny, waving little specks of black.

I can't believe that this big important part of my life appears to be over.

A lump comes up in my throat.

I miss them already.

Dad's thrown my stepmother out of the house. He's invited Heather to move in, but she wants to 'keep her independence' for a while longer so they're going to stay living next door to one another.

On the night we get home I unpack all my clothes. I hang them with spaces in between but I manage not to use the ruler to measure four centimetres.

'There,' I say, surveying my handiwork.

I skip downstairs and do only ten jumps on the top stair and another ten at the bottom.

Dad's outside trying to light the coals in the barbecue even though it's spitting with rain.

'Hello, Princess,' he says. My heart flips over with pain and love.

'Dad,' I say. 'I wish you'd told me about the drinking. I could have helped.'

Dad puts down his wide selection of gas lighters, petrol cans, fish slices and tongs and turns round.

A small wisp of black smoke wends its way towards my head. *Dirt Alert*. I duck.

'How could I?' he says. 'You had enough on your plate. And, anyway, I was too ashamed to admit I had a problem. I'm supposed to be the strong one, remember?'

'I think you're strong,' I say. I saw Dad tip all his bottles of wine and beer down the sink when we got home from the hospital. It took about three hours, but he had a grim, determined look in his eye.

It's pouring now so Dad abandons the barbecue idea and we go inside. He cooks semi-frozen chicken fillets in batter and burns the oven chips and we drink a toast with fizzy lemonade.

'Mum would laugh at you,' I say. 'She always said that you could burn air.'

'Your mother said a lot of things,' said Dad. 'Some of them were true. Others were complete fabrication. She was a lunatic, but I miss her.'

We're standing in the lounge in front of that long mirror with the black frame and the gold swirls.

'I'm chucking it out tomorrow,' says Dad, reading my mind.

I look at our reflections. I see a pretty teenager in a long red tiered skirt, very long red dangly earrings and with cool dark swishy hair.

Behind her stands a big-built, bear-like man with floppy brown hair wearing a red-checked shirt.

Dad's almost touching me, but not quite.

There's a great big smear bang in the centre of the mirror.

Uh-oh. *Dirt Alert.*

He's watching me watching the smear.

'Don't worry, Dad,' I say. 'I can control my OCD better now. I'll leave it alone.'

He goes off to get an overcooked apple pie and I start to follow.

Then I stop.

I make a mental note of where the smudge is, for later.

Just in case.

Acknowledgements

Many thanks to my agent, Peter Buckman, for his infectious enthusiasm on this project, and to Leah Thaxton and the team at Egmont for making work seem like pleasure. Also love and thanks to Sarah Stovell and Sue Fox.

EGMONT PRESS: ETHICAL PUBLISHING

Egmont Press is about turning writers into successful authors and children into passionate readers – producing books that enrich and entertain. As a responsible children's publisher, we go even further, considering the world in which our consumers are growing up.

Safety First
Naturally, all of our books meet legal safety requirements. But we go further than this; every book with play value is tested to the highest standards – if it fails, it's back to the drawing-board.

Made Fairly
We are working to ensure that the workers involved in our supply chain – the people that make our books – are treated with fairness and respect.

Responsible Forestry
We are committed to ensuring all our papers come from environmentally and socially responsible forest sources.

**For more information, please visit our website at
www.egmont.co.uk/ethical**

Mixed Sources
Product group from well-managed
forests and other controlled sources
www.fsc.org Cert no. TT-COC-002332
© 1996 Forest Stewardship Council

Egmont is passionate about helping to preserve the world's remaining ancient forests. We only use paper from legal and sustainable forest sources, so we know where every single tree comes from that goes into every paper that makes up every book.

This book is made from paper certified by the Forestry Stewardship Council (FSC), an organisation dedicated to promoting responsible management of forest resources. For more information on the FSC, please visit **www.fsc.org**. To learn more about Egmont's sustainable paper policy, please visit **www.egmont.co.uk/ethical**.